Toads in Tank Suits

Fran Jones

Toads in Tank Suits

A Tandem of Talent

Frances L. Jones

VANTAGE PRESS
New York

Published by Vantage Press, Inc.
516 West 34th Street, New York, New York 10001

Manufactured in the United States of America
ISBN: 0-533-13284-3

Library of Congress Catalog Card No.: 99-96653

0 9 8 7 6 5 4 3 2 1

To those great Sea Sprite members and Aquarius
swimmers from Michigan

Note: Credit is to the girls I coached in the Sea Sprite club
and the Aquarius club.

Contents

Introduction

Many people say swimming should be the "in" thing for kids living on a planet of seventy percent water. I agree. After learning to walk, my greatest accomplishment was learning to swim. I'd cheer and shout whoopee if every child could swim like a fish.

It's just a coincidence that I was born under the sign of Aquarius, but for as long as I can remember, water has meant pure happiness.

Beginning in the bathtub, swirling the water and splashing the waves were a delight, the reasons to screech and squeal.

With my dad's help, at bath time I learned to float and flutter kick. After Dad built my pool, speed swimming became my passion. Under his coaching, I swam for four years in the ten-and-under little kids classification. My mom kept a log of the hours I spent in the wet stuff during those years. Nearly two thousand hours were enough to turn this minnow into a flying fish.

Toads in Tank Suits is a story of my swimming career. It flows with fun, friends, and family. Let's pop the starter's gun and dive into a wet tale that begins with a nymph and ends with a teenage synchronized swimmer who wanted to be a United States champion in the duet class.

Toads in Tank Suits

I

Ools and Pools

As a tadpole of five years, just before a bath, running around in my pink, naked body was more fun than eating chocolate candy. After the tub was filled with warm water, I slapped and stirred the wet stuff until the mirror steamed and the walls dripped. I was the cause of those puddles Mom had to soak up.

A bath was a party of shouts and spouts, giggles and wiggles.

"Ash arty, ash arty," I squealed, unable to say splash party because I couldn't pronounce S and PL together. When I climbed into the warm soft bubbles, Mom was there at the tub-side. Slosh, splatter, splat. The bathroom became flood stage.

"Hold still," she pleaded, wiping a drizzle off her nose. "The next time I give you a scrub, I'll be wearing your dad's wet suit."

Determined to show Mom what I had learned from Dad, I caught a breath, lay face down, and began to flutter kick.

"Stop! Stop!" she shouted. "Don't try your skills with me. Save 'em for your dad. He's the one who wants you to become a swimmer." Blotting the wet stuff on her neck and chest, Mom grumbled, "Water was meant to be a thirst quencher and save a life, so don't try to drown me to death."

From puddles to pools, my mom feared the water. A phobia, the doctor called it. A condition seldom overcome.

While squirting and squirming around in the tub, my body was slippery to scrub. Wiggling and giggling and screeching for more, I splashed the bathroom from ceiling to floor. Poor Mom lost her beauty parlor blow-dry. Strings of wet hair stuck to her face and water came trickling down her ribs. Pinching her nose, she tried to hold back the sniffles, but a sneezing fit followed. Not once, but twice and then again.

"C. J., oh, C. J." she hollered. Those initials stood for my dad, Charles Jacobs. "I need help with Julie," she pleaded.

Julie Jacobs. That's me. Dad's only minnow.

"Julie's ool, Julie's ool," I kept shouting in total ecstasy.

"No, not yet," said Dad. "Your new pool will be in the backyard. When spring arrives, tractors will come and dig the hole. For now, learn to kick and blow bubbles in this bathtub."

"Julie's ool," I screeched, claiming it to be mine and not to belong to those other make-believe kids I played with.

"Let me finish here, Lori," said Dad to Mom. "Julie needs another swim lesson. Before long, she's going to swim like a fish. I guarantee it."

"Oh, Chuck," complained Mom. "I'm sure Julie will be your darling mermaid, but a backyard pool will by my pain in the neck. The entire idea is a deadly nightmare for me." Pitching a wet towel into Dad's midsection, she left the room muttering, "Outright dangerous and unreasonable."

As the days grew longer and the grass turned green, the pool builders arrived. Stacks of fat sacks, piles of dirt, an engine that puffed white paste, and of course, a scoop shovel occupied my backyard.

"I'm taking no chances," said Mom, locking the doors and fitting safety seals over the knobs. "I'm warning you,

2

Chuck, if Julie goes near that hole while you are at the office, I'll call the paramedics."

Dad was great at changing Mom's mood before she became overstressed with disastrous thoughts.

"I'll set up a play station for Julie in front of our big window," he offered. "Let her be entertained by a real live back yard video. Go get your stuffed swimmers, Julie. They can watch, too."

A rumble, rumble, roar filled the air, rattling the house. The scoop shovel's engine was warming up before biting big chunks out of the yard.

I ran to the window carrying my stuffed toys: a gray-and-white shark, which I held in my teeth, a yellow orange octopus, a black-and-white penguin, and a smiling dolphin.

By lunchtime the dirt piles were tall pyramids and the back yard hole seemed deep enough to swallow our family van.

Day after day, I watched and played by the window.

"Julie's ool, Julie's ool," echoed through the house. Pretending my dolphin could leap the waves, I ran with it, back and forth in front of the window. A worker noticed my playful mood. He held his nose and pretended to sink. We giggled together.

One day the workmen arrived wearing hard hats and boots. They attached a fire hose to the engine that puffed white paste.

"Let her go," came the command. Two men held the hose. A stream of white mud blew into the belly of my pool. Other workmen waded into the goo and smoothed it until the pool sides and its bottom were covered.

"Look, Mommy," I shouted. "Frosting in my ool. Yum-yum frosting." It looked so good I licked the window. Mom's face gathered laughing wrinkles. For a moment she seemed to enjoy the back yard scene.

"Frosting instead of chlorine-flavored water sounds delightful to me," she said. "Sugar tastes better than bleach anytime. But Julie, the white stuff isn't frosting. It's gunite and is as hard as our cement sidewalk. It won't melt in your mouth."

I was sure I had seen frosting and expected my pool to taste as sweet as candy.

By midsummer the pool was finished. A white fence protected my big tub and a serpentine deck was where Dad parked my new floatable toys.

"Let's have a splash party," Dad suggested, with a heart-lifting tone in his voice. "We will invite a handful of girls from Julie's kindergarten class."

"I suppose you want a pool-opening celebration," said Mom, "a midsummer christening of that deep dark hole."

"Exactly!" exclaimed Dad. "Perfect idea." Seeing his chance to coach aquatic skills, he added, "I'd like nothing better than to start those little nymphs off on a swimming career." With a gleaming glance at me, he asked, "How does that sound to you, Miss Mermaid?"

Starting in my fingers, a tingle tickled all through my body parts.

"Splash party, Dad. Splash party," I cheered, pronouncing the words as if I never before had trouble with S and PL. Running toward my dad, I was caught up in a hugging embrace.

The day of my party, Mom tied clusters of balloons on the pool fence, but she didn't go near the water.

Megan, Cori, Mo, and Leyla arrived in their bikinis. I wore a red, white, and blue tank suit with "All America" printed across the front. The suit was Dad's choice. He called it his firecracker. I loved the shooting stars that burst across the back. Leyla claimed my new salmon-colored sea horse and rode it around in the shallow water. Dad called her Lady Godiva for some reason. Megan stood with her feet glued to the deck. She was afraid like my mom. Mo, Cori, and I climbed into my saucer. Dad's big muscles set our tube spinning. We hung tightly to the saucer even though he tried his best to spill us overboard. When we all, except Megan, became water-soaked with wrinkled skin and blue lips, Dad gave us each a flutter board.

"Hold your board and kick across the pool," he directed, with a demonstration. "You need to warm up." Pointing his finger at Megan, he added, "Your job is to life guard and watch very closely." Inflating her lungs with the importance of her assignment, Megan seemed to lose her fear. From that time on, she wore a smile.

My kick rumbled like Dad had taught me in the bathtub. Cori, Mo, and Leyla kicked high above the water, their skinny legs thrashing.

"No, not in the air," hollered Dad. "Don't make this drill look like an explosion in a toothpick factory."

Going back and forth across the pool until Dad was satisfied had us gasping for breath.

"We'll finish this splash party with the cannonball plop," said Dad. "Line up on deck. Jump in, one at a time with your knees in your arms. Make a tight ball. I'll catch you."

"Let me go first, let me, Dad," I teased. "I'll show 'em how." With my toes clamped over the pool edge, I gave a mighty leap. My knees hit my stomach, knocking out all my air. The pool swallowed me in one gulp and I kept sinking. Dad didn't catch me when I expected it. From the bottom of the pool, I saw his nearest leg and scrambled for it. Finally, his arm gave me a lift.

The christening splash party ended when Mom called us inside for treats. Her hot sharp-flavored pizza warmed our quivering bodies and her mix of juices turned our tongues red. We all sat in a happy huddle on the front steps waiting for Mo's mother, bragging that we were now swimmers. All, that is, except Megan.

"Maybe next time," she said, in not too promising a voice.

During my little-girl years, Dad was my coach. Learning from him sent shivers of pleasure waving through my body. He showed me how and explained how to swim four different racing strokes. From his constant shower of compliments, I gained confidence.

"Great form, phenomenal talent. You're a natural," he said in a genuine convincing tone.

After my seventh birthday, he launched me into a practice schedule Mom complained about. Dad wanted me in an Olympic-size pool for serious training. We swam distances in the Y pool, at school pools, and in the community center. When Mom realized what was happening, her complaints were too late. Dad had purchased a stopwatch, a video camera, goggles for me, and three new tank suits.

"Now see here, Charles," she said. "Julie needs time to enjoy other activities. Dancing and the children's theater would be wonderful. They develop poise, stage presence, and keep young minds veiled in fantasy. She can't be both a speed swimmer and an actress. Besides, if she swims, her eyes will be red, her hair will bleach, and she'll smell like chlorine."

Mom's flood of reasons nearly drowned Dad.

"All right," he said. "Ask Julie what she wants to do." Mom's face drained of color and she slumped into a chair.

"I know the answer and so do you," she moaned. "Just tell me when and where our daughter will compete?"

Dad entered me in the ten-and-under age group competition. I was the skinniest kid in the lanes and my big feet were like anchors. My tumble turns were spastic looking, but Dad never chewed me out for the things I couldn't do. After each race he'd say, "You are rhythm in motion, Julie."

I was hooked on speed swimming and had shoeboxes of medals.

Yes, I ran around with red eyes, flaky skin, and a chlorine scent.

II

Aquabatics

Shortly after entering the fourth grade, I fell in love with synchronized swimming. While watching the Summer Olympics on television, my mind set like a dropped anchor on swimming to music. It looked so awesome, so neat, and so super.

"I want to join a sync club," I announced to Mom. Horror at the word "sync" froze her straight as a pencil.

"A what club?" she shrieked, her fear of the water returning like the tide.

"You know, Mom. Swimming to music. I'd die to try that sport. It's incredible!"

Swimming and dying sounded synonymous to Mom. Her chin set firm and flat. I expected her to scream no. Instead, she spoke in a wailful voice.

"It's water, water, water, with you. Are wet tank suits and swim medals worth all your time? If you take up that sport, there won't be a moment's rest for any of us. When I was in college, we called that kind of swimming, water ballet. First came the search for music, then a routine to choreograph. The biggest headache was making a costume that would fit after it got wet."

That's where I came in.

Whammo! It hit me. "MOTHER," I shouted. "We can

do synchro together. You've always designed my clothes and you can teach dance. Come on, Mom. You'd be perfect."

Mom had been a designer of toddler's clothing. After I came along, her creations filled my closet with everything from playsuits to fancy Easter dresses. She was a dancer too, a charter member of Orchesis, her college dance club.

Mom's puckered face relaxed just thinking of those good old days. The challenge to teach me her skills was tempting, but she was cautious. Looking me straight in the eyes, her words stung with doubt.

"Don't be too sure Dad will agree to your new ripple. He is bursting with pride over your success in speed swimming."

"Oh, Mom," I sobbed, feeling a cramp in my plan. "He'll go for it, won't he?"

"When he comes home, you do the convincing," she said. "I'll just listen."

That evening our house resembled a gymnastics classroom. Determined to show Dad what synchro looked like, I somersaulted, tried the splits, did backbends, and leaped crossing my legs in mid-air. Dad watching, kept shaking his head, and laughing.

"All right, jumping bean," he shouted. "Stop before you dislocate a joint."

Whirling like a merry-go-round, I waited for his O.K.

"There is a private club in our area known as the Aquarius club. Its reputation is top class. Girls who are members train the year around. They compete in the national championships and a few go on to the Olympic trials. I'll ask the coach if she has an opening in the beginner's class. You'll qualify because of your great swimming skill. Try synchro for a year. If you don't like the sport, you may return to speed."

No longer could I stand on earth. My insides exploded

with happiness. Even Mom joined in, showing as much excitement as a mother bird shows over the hatching of her first egg.

"I will teach you the techniques of dancing and help you interpret the mystery music conceals," she announced. "I'll guarantee rapid progress, if Dad will hang mirrors in our games room. We must be able to see ourselves in action."

"TERRIFIC! WHAT A DEAL!" I shouted, feeling like I think the Olympic winners feel when their flag goes up the pole.

Dad signed me up for synchro and agreed to drive me to class three nights a week.

"Remember, Julie," he said. "Synchro is a unique sport much like diving and figure skating. You won't race to beat the clock, you'll be convincing a panel of highly trained technicians."

"No problem, Dad. I'm going for it," I cheered.

Lesson number one actually had me doubting my switch from speed to synchro. Nothing was familiar except the warm-up laps. The coach expected we all could float on our back.

"Take a layout with your arms stretched above your head," she hollered. "In that position float like a cork." In no way did my skinny body and big feet keep me afloat. So I failed, slowly sinking feet first.

"Line up at the trough," she ordered. "Hold the trough, legs in the air, toes pointed. I want you to press your body under until your back is against the wall."

Catching a breath, I did it but smacked my head against the pool side. Water rampaged through my sinuses and I came up snorting. The coach kept on giving commands. I just watched.

"Stretch, suck in your stomach. Lock your knees.

Squeeze your buttocks. Get comfy upside down, you toads. This position is vertical."

Holding my breath in an upside down position was not my thing. Dad had taught me rhythmic breathing while in a horizontal position.

"What a bummer," I said, feeling stupid.

The gallon of water running from my nose made me sneeze. Noticing my dilemma, the coach stopped instruction, came over to me carrying a weird-looking clamp.

"We wear nose clips in synchro," she said. "You'll need several of these. Always carry a spare in the leg of your tank suit."

Class instruction moved on to a strange arm movement called sculling.

"The most important skill," said the coach. "You will use it for support and for propulsion. Assume a layout on your back, arms at your sides. Flatten and stretch your hands. Swing the forearms away from and back toward the hips. The pattern is about the width of a computer paper. Your fingers will loop as you swing in and out."

I tried what she demonstrated on deck. It didn't work. My arms were trained for stroking.

"Go the pool distance," she ordered.

I didn't move an inch. My hands just sputtered and churned up a few waves. Dad's star swimmer was a dead duck in the water. In my mind, the whole lesson was a disaster.

On the way home, Dad was anxious to hear my story.

"Well, Dad," I announced, "so far this sport isn't synchronized anything. Aquabatics fits what I've been doing."

"I hope you didn't expect this sport to be an easy wash," he said.

"Not exactly," I answered. "It sure looked real easy on

11

TV, but now I know it's worse than swimming with an anchor tied to my leg."

Lesson number two was the miracle lesson. I was instructed to stand waist high in nine feet of water.

"Head for the deep end," hollered the coach. "Stand and face me. Move your legs in a whirling eggbeater pattern. This is a half out and half in exercise."

Her deck demo reminded me of a cowboy sitting astraddle his horse with his legs flinging.

"Get uplift from your leg action. I mean waist high."

My legs circled and twisted until they became as useless as melted butter.

"Waist high. She's kidding. Impossible," I mouthed quietly.

The coach plunged ahead with still more impossible moves.

"Get that eggbeater down cold, then add expressive arm movements. Look up and copy me," she shouted. "Arms must talk. They are your interpreter."

"There is something new every day," I told Mom. "My coach is teaching effortlessness and gracefulness. I'm clumsy and awkward. How about some tips?"

Mom knew where to begin and where to end. She stood me in front of the mirror so often, I thought my image was alive.

"Ease into a pattern," she said. "Slowly finish the movement." I copied her gracefulness until I became like her shadow.

I loved controlling my body on land or in the water. It took almost two more years to master the basic skills of synchro. Finally, I became a rare water creature. I could sit near the top of the water with both legs in the air. Sculling made that position possible. Pressing to vertical felt weird, but I lined up like a north-south compass arrow to support a few ballet leg positions while upside down. The awful eggbeater kick began to smooth out until I became tired, then I bounced like a bobber in rough water.

"The coach keeps pouring it on," I told Mom. "Every swimmer has been given a stick figure handbook to study. I have to learn graphic designs called figures. For next year's competition, I'll need a repertoire of figures that have a difficulty from 1.5 through 1.8. For better or worse, I'm going to face that panel of experts Dad told me about."

It was hopeless to talk to people about my sport because I didn't make sense. My language wrinkled their faces. The crane, the heron, and the flamingo were birds to them, but to me, those names were water positions.

Dad helped coach me through the simple figures. Together, we watched videos that had been taken from an underwater window. He had a super eye for technique. Over and over, he analyzed body line, support sculling, and speed of action. Then one day he burned out.

"This is as exciting as watching grass grow," he jollied. "Those national judges must have fathoms of patience."

I was as happy as a clam in high water when fall practice took off in high gear. Helen Zavitz, my new coach, was on deck. Her plan for me couldn't have been better. I became a member of the Taco Tango Team.

"At last, I'm swimming to music," I cheered.

The tango routine turned Mom on like a floodlight. When she heard I would swim a Latin-American theme, she called Mrs. Z and volunteered to choreograph the deck dance and the arm movements appropriate for the water. Our house turned into a live dance studio. Mom was either dancing in the kitchen or checking her proud poses in the mirror. Her steps and body language were authentically Latin-American. There were dips and glides, sharp head turns, clicks of the fingers, and a fan float. All of these fit the music.

Mom insisted the 3T swimmers, that's what we called our routine, learn the rhumba and the tango, and have fun with the Cha-cha-cha. Her job was to make us look good from the waist up. Our job was to mix her beautiful moves with that homely, clumsy eggbeater kick.

Like a classroom professor's, Mom's demonstration and word-pictures were very clear.

"An arm movement begins just above the water surface. The air-borne pattern has width and height. No matter what pattern you have chosen, the arm must reach a high focal point above the surface. The hand follows the arm. Hold an imaginary toothpick, end to end, between your thumb and second finger. The fingers, then become attractive, graceful additions to the arm design."

It was cool to watch Mom and the team in the mirror. After an hour of serious dancing, we broke up, made weird faces at each other, and giggled.

Mrs. Z, Mom, and the 3T girls had a winning routine. We competed in the Midwest against other Junior Olympic athletes. Our scores kept improving. We brought home bronze, silver, and finally gold!

III

A Sporting Chance

"Today is the day I feel like announcing my good news to the world," I shouted. "I'm a teenager. That's cool." Bouncing the dance steps Mom had taught me (entrechats, jetés, and pirouettes), I went leaping and flying about. Mom bolted into my room not sure if I was sick, mad, or happy.

"Are you rehearsing or what?" she asked.

"No, I'm celebrating. Finally I'm old enough to compete in nationals. You know, Mom, a few girls are champions at age thirteen. I want that chance, too."

Mom's eyes flashed like two polished nuggets.

"I'm sure you have the talent, Julie. Why don't you try solo swimming? You're a prima donna to me."

"No, Mom. A soloist is a special genius, a top notcher on her own. I want a partner. I'd love to win the duet nationals."

"What's all the racket up here?" asked Dad, as he entered my room with the newspaper under his arm.

"Julie wants to swim tandem, Chuck. I suggested solo," answered Mom.

"Well, Julie is right," said Dad. "If her sport is really synchronized swimming, she should compete with a partner or a team. Probably Esther Williams was the reason for the solo event to hit the sports world. She was a fast backstroker Hollywood made into a movie star. They dressed

15

her in glitter and plumes, made sets of Roman spas, and staged fountains in the center of a huge pool. You know, girls. The works. Everyone thought she was King Neptune's daughter."

"Water show stuff, huh, Dad?"

"Esther's aquatic movies were good entertainment, and she made big bucks during her career," he answered.

"I'll settle for big medals and the title champion," I said, with a wish in my heart and twinkling eyes. "I have more good news to tell you. My coach wants all her swimmers to see the national duet championships coming next month to Detroit."

"Wonderful!" exclaimed Mom. "We'll all go. I'd like to see your future competition."

I lost nights of sleep waiting for the nationals. The days lingered on until my count was down to one. At last, I'd see a pair of U.S. champions up close and live.

Loads of Michigan's swimmers were there the night of the finals. Dad, Mom, and I sat perched high in the balcony above the pool. Dad, fumbling with his camcorder, blurted, "This is the show of shows. Right, Julie?"

Jiggling like a hot teakettle, I wanted to whistle but decided not to. Instead, I urged Dad to get set. "Catch the opening ceremonies, Dad. Please shoot the works."

Almost as if I had given the signal, drums snared and trumpets blared. The room darkened except for the spotlight on the American flag. A deep voice said, "Please stand for the national anthem." I popped up like a mushroom on a damp hillside. My heart thumped so hard I felt wobbly. By the time the anthem finished, I was moist all over. Lights flooded the room, giving us a clear view.

The walls of the natatorium were draped with patriotic bunting. In poses like Greek gods, the trophies stood on a table of purple velvet. Pillars of floral bouquets outlined the door marked "contestant's entry."

"WOW! Mom," I shrieked. "Look at those two macho guys in tuxes standing by the competitor's door. Do they get to kiss the winners or what?"

"No, silly. They are the escorts." Focusing her binoculars, she added in a voice of acclamation, "They are handsome. I take it you've discovered boys."

Five judges in white uniforms sat in ladder highchairs with their pencils poised to evaluate each performance.

"This is really big time," I said, boastfully. "Someday I'll stand on the winner's platform and see my image in the water."

"Take it one stroke at a time," said Dad. "Anything is possible if you try hard enough, stick to it, and have good luck along the way."

Closing my eyes, I fancied my moment. I saw the gold medal. I heard the crowd cheering and I felt the hugs from my fans. The vision was so real, I hollered right out loud, "I WANT TO BE A CHAMPION."

The fans around me gaped and laughed. One broad-chested guy shouted, "Miracles happen. Make a wish, Aphrodite, and toss in a coin." I pulled my head in like a turtle and settled deep in my seat. Slowly, with one eye, I glanced at the guy's rosy face.

"Who's he? King Neptune?" I asked Dad over the back of my hand.

"Some bullfrog who thinks his croak is musical," came the reply. I was snickering when the room grew quiet except for the veil-like waterfall at the trough. The drains gurgled after swallowing the overflow. Beady red eyes and long noses of the television cameras appeared on deck and moved into position to catch the action.

"Welcome to the Senior National Duets for synchronized swimmers," said the man with a round face.

"I've seen him on TV," I squealed. "He's the anchor for ABC's 'Wide World of Sports.' He was the commentator for the games the year I decided to join the Aquarius club. Remember, Dad? I was about eight years old. Just a polliwog."

"Oh, yes. I remember how crazy you were to dance on the water. You couldn't wait to learn those stunts with crazy names. Like ga-vee-ta, or however you say it."

"It's ga-veh-ah-tah," I answered, accenting each syllable.

"With all this pomp and circumstance, you won't be satisfied until you have a national crown," said Dad.

Flinging my arms airborne, I cheered, "That's me. One year from now when the nationals are held, I want to enter."

The contestants' door opened and two girls with wading-bird legs moved to their starting positions.

"Ladies and gentlemen, I present duet number one, the white doves," said the announcer.

Like a sponge, I absorbed their dazzling appearance.

"Fabulous, Mom. How about those costumes?"

Each dove was wearing a one-piece white chiffon suit. Scattered across the bust line were faceted zircons, beads, and sequins, all arranged in a winglike design. The headpiece was awesome; an iridescent finial of sequins and feathers.

Slipping to the edge of my seat, I waited for the music to begin. A lilting melody of a single horn sent me soaring into space. Gradually the music climbed to the dynamic power of a full symphony. Recognizing the tune, I hummed along, absorbing the choreography from my fingertips to my toes. I had no intention of disturbing King Neptune, but he winked at me as I glanced at him.

"What a flirt," I whispered. "He's watching me."

The amplified music made Dad want to howl like a dog. I saw him plug his ears for relief. At that moment the doves thrust airborne in a vertical maneuver resembling a rocket. Piercing upward, legs first, then opening into the splits, they wrapped their legs and spun out of sight.

"What a vortex," I cheered, remembering my coach's exact word for that movement.

As the music calmed, Dad shared his observations. "I know how you get to nationals, Julie. You must be half fish. I can't tell when these girls breathe. This duo is Guinness material."

"We're underwater about half the time, Dad, so we catch air whenever."

While chewing my nose clip necklace, I watched with a devouring eye, twenty duets. As the last pair posed on deck, I slipped my wet clips onto my nose.

"Wish I could swim with those girls," I said to Mom.

"Looks like you are ready," she answered, smiling at my pinched nose.

In a nasal tone, I agreed. "I'm going to make a big ripple in this sport, Mom. Wait and see."

The electronic scoreboard flashed the results. The doves took first. I clapped until my hands were red.

Dad helped me to accept the outcome of any competition.

"These swimmers are all winners," he said, "or they wouldn't be here. They have won self-discipline, found loyalty, know how to respect the body, and have given up other pleasures to be an achiever. So you see, Julie, it isn't just winning that counts, it's how you play the game."

"Basically, Dad, you are telling me the Olympic slogan. Mrs. Z broadcasts those catchwords into her mike every practice. She says they help keep us focused."

King Neptune disappeared as we left the balcony.

Heading for home, we motored along an expressway. Dad asked, "What's your future, Julie? Have you told Mrs. Zavitz how you feel about duets?"

"I think she has a plan for me. She knows I'd go ape to have a partner."

As our car rolled to a stop in the driveway, I recognized a blue-and-white van parked by the road. I had traveled across the Midwest in that four-wheeler.

"So, what's the blue bubble doing here?" I hollered.

Mrs. Zavitz stepped out of the car. She was a petite woman about five feet tall, weighing a drop over one hundred pounds. Her manner was strict, a feisty coach who demanded maximum effort from her swimmers. She and a handful of other American coaches pioneered synchro. Developing its beginning as an art form to the present Olympic sport; took nearly thirty years.

"Hello, Julie," she hollered. "Some contest, didn't you think? The doves were superior, definitely worth the highest score."

"Incredible," I answered. "Neat choreography and unbelievable execution. I'd die to swim like that."

"Please come in," said Mom. "I'd like to hear your critique of the meet."

"I came to discuss your daughter's future," said Mrs. Z. "I have a plan."

My heart flipped. I swallowed but nothing went down. My eyes popped. I wanted to scream, Oh, my God, but it caught in my throat. Then I flushed tomato red.

"Come, sit down, everyone," said Dad, who by now had noticed my condition.

"I know your interest in duets, Julie," said Mrs. Z. "Would you like a chance to complete in that division?"

"WOULD I! You better believe it."

"Well then," said Mrs. Z, "it is a big step that I'm suggesting and one that will get your flutter kick rumbling." A grin of surprise filled her face. "I propose you become a partner with Sandy Jenkins."

"SANDY JENKINS?" I screamed, holding my ribs and coiling like a worm. "Sandy is famous. She's in the elite class and I'm only a junior team swimmer. She's our national solo champion."

"Well now," said Mrs. Z, "it may seem as if I"m asking the swan to teach her cygnet to swim, but not so. You already have great talent and the temperament to be an achiever. Of course, I have discussed this with Sandy. She's ecstatic. If you girls progress rapidly, there is a chance you could enter next year's nationals."

Beaming with pride, Dad said, "I'll drive the six P.M. taxi to the pool for free." With that, Mom hid her emotions by sniffing and snorting her happiness into her handkerchief.

"Fine. I'm expecting great waves. Congratulations to all of you and best of luck," said Mrs. Z, as she swept up her briefcase and made her way out the door.

"We thank you for your confidence in our daughter," offered Dad, bowing like an English nobleman before closing the door.

"MAN, OH MAN! WHAT A CHANGE! Am I gonna sink or swim this routine?" I shouted.

"Rub-a-dub-dub, you're deep in the tub," teased Dad. "Either hoist your sail or start your motor, young lady. Your race has begun."

Spinning upward on my toes, I went soaring through the house like a gossamer-winged butterfly.

IV

Ace Partners

"I have a craving, Dad, for a pet. It's not that I've outgrown my stuffed toys, but I want something live, real and cool. I know we can't have hairy creatures like a cat or dog 'cause Mom is allergic to fur. Hit me with some ideas, Dad."

"At the speed you've been flying these days," answered Dad. "You need a pilot's license, not a pet to take care of."

"Come on, Dad. Give me a break."

"Well then. Buy a cocoon. Watch it turn into a butterfly, or grow ladybugs in a glass display chest," he said.

"You've got to be kidding. Those are slow movers, the creepy-crawler type. I want a speedy pet."

My mind sorted through the kingdoms of surf and turf. Finally I landed a big one.

"Fish," I announced explosively. "Those guys are good swimmers, have catchy choreography, and wear cool costumes. I'll buy an aquarium, get some coral and sea grass. How about it, Dad? Could you set up the tank in my room?"

"Sure," he answered, "but you'll need to ask Mom. Better prepare a convincing case before you present your plan to her."

When Mom came home from the beauty parlor, I spilled the works.

"My room needs a face lift, Mom. I don't want speed

swimming clippings and medals on the walls. Dad said he could set up an aquarium for me. I really want pet fish."

"Oh, Julie. Another tank of water right under my nose," she complained. "I suffered over the pool. Must I listen to gurgling water night and day?"

"Please, Mom," I coaxed. "I'll keep it all in my room." Exhaling her fear of water and the annoyance I presented, she gave her consent without a warning this time, probably because I was a teenager too big to drown in a fish tank.

Dad and I made a trip to the pet shop. I went bananas over two yellow and blue polka dot beauties imported from China. Squashing my nose against their tank, I said, "You two are perfect look alike partners, the way I want to look with Sandy. I need more curves. I'm too flat and skinny. I'm a domino chip. She's the Miss America type. What I need is a metamorphic miracle. Wish I were anything but a bean pole."

The next day Dad set up the aquarium in my room. As I poured my two fish into the tank, I gave each a name.

"You are Jake," I said, hoping he was a he, "and you are Jude, no matter what." They darted and dashed through the stalagmite coral finding places to hide.

I didn't want to hide. I wanted to see Sandy. She had gone to Florida for a solo invitational meet, so I was waiting for her to call. Waiting way too long. My eyes were dancing in circles and my finger couldn't resist the telephone dial. I punched SYNCHRO, Sandy's private number. A recording answered. "Toads Inc. I'm practicing in deep water. Leave your name and number. When I come up for air, I'll call."

At last, she was home and probably at the pool for open swimming. Tossing a kiss at Jake and Jude, I grabbed my clips and swim bag. The pool was just a five-minute pedal on my bike. I knew the path by heart. The bumps and toys on the sidewalk were easy to avoid.

Opening the door to the dressing room, a hot cloud of steam puffed into my face. I headed toward a locker. One was wide open with my name in letters taped to the door.

"What's this?" I screamed. "Who's playing tricks?"

A giant playing card, the ace of hearts dangled from a hook. An attached note said, "I've been dealt an ace partner. We'll win gold together."

Jumping out of my clothes and into my suit. I fast-stepped to the pool. There at the deep end, Sandy was upside down practicing a difficult figure. I recognized her feet, arched like a rainbow and twisting on toe point. I just knew it was Sandy.

Leaving the deck, I flew like a javelin, puncturing the water next to her. Sinking to the depth of her head so that she could see me, I pulled my ears and made a freakish face. Like an octopus, she wrapped me in her arms and held tightly until we hit bottom. Pushing off, we boiled to the surface spouting like whales. With shrieks of happiness, our arms wrapped again and we sank like an anchor tossed overboard.

The life guard thought he was seeing a double drowning. Yanking the shephard's crook off the wall, he mounted the diving board and plunged the pole into the water. Hooking us, he pulled with all his might. Up we flew like sailfish in the Atlantic.

"Get this hook off," screamed Sandy, wrenching her body in all directions. With that, the guard realized we were fooling. His face turned uglier than a distempered dog's. Hammering his finger at us, he shouted, "OUT" more clearly than an umpire at a baseball game.

"I didn't mean to cause trouble," I groaned, lowering half of my face in the water like a crocodile.

"That's okay partner," whispered Sandy as she turned

her back to the guard. "He's probably a new graduate from life-saving class. We freaked him out."

Feeling sheepish, we swam halfhearted breast strokes toward the shallow end. In spite of our encounter with the lifeguard, we wanted to talk synchro.

"Get dressed, partner," said Sandy. "Let's blow this steam bath and head for my house. We have some catching up to do."

"I'm riding wheels," I said. "Are you?"

Sandy was quick to answer. "I bike every place. It's part of my training."

After tussling with the mix of moist bodies and dry jeans, we mounted our wheels and started to spin toward Sandy's. We whizzed through the mall parking and pumped up a hill. Sandy was a half block ahead of me. She was an engine of steel. When I coasted around a corner into a block of town houses, my breathing was five times faster than it is after a swim routine.

Sandy took me into her lofty place and up a winding stairwell. Oodles of framed pictures dappled the wall. In a jumpy voice, I teased, "Is this the Swimming Hall of Fame?" Sandy answered with a giggle.

"You are looking at my career in pictures. Once you're a champion, photographers swarm around like bees. It's worse than being a New York model. I'm never sure when a camera is pointed at me."

"Who's the character in these shots?" I asked, pointing to a collage of photos.

With a regretful groan, Sandy answered, "My greatest embarrassment. These were taken at the Canadian International in Quebec. That's me in costume. I'm D'Artagnan, the Musketeer. See the plume in my hat. Pretty classy looking on deck, but when I hit the water, the feathers drooped like the tail of a shaggy dog. When I surfaced, one eye was covered shut. Poor Mrs. Z was mortified. Just for fun, we renamed the routine the Pirate. I'll never swim it again."

Sandy launched into the deck choreography, hollering, "Give me some stomping rhythm, partner, and watch D'Artagnan strut his stuff."

I was dying of dumbness and couldn't begin to pronounce the musketeer's name, but I could move my feet, so there on the steps I stomped like a stiff-legged tin soldier.

"Show me more, partner," I coaxed.

Pointing to a lineup of pictures, Sandy continued, "These photos were taken at Balboa Park in California. I was costumed to represent Quicksilver, Mercury's messenger. My mom spent weeks sewing silver sequins all over my suit."

"WOW! What a glitter trip," I exclaimed.

"Not really," answered Sandy. "Mom and I kept the costume a secret from Mrs. Zavitz. We wanted it to be a surprise. Well, when she saw me swimming in the prelims, my water line was low, I mean low. The suit weighed a ton. As I finished, an official whispered in my ear, 'You needed a ring buoy, young lady.' "

"You died. You must have died," I shrieked.

"Mrs. Z was really mad. She steamed at me for two days. For the finals, I had to wear a spandex suit of feather weight. Never will Mom and I design a costume surprise. Mrs. Z told us to discard our water show ideas and think sport, not stage."

Sandy tugged at my arm.

"Come on, Jacobs. You have to see my room."

Dozens of friendly faces greeted me on poster-size paper.

"These are past champions," said Sandy. "Just to look at them gives me fighting power."

Turning a slow three-sixty, breathing fits of surprise,

the room of memorabilia overwhelmed my widening eyes. Licking my lips at Sandy's case of medals, I could taste victory. Those round disks, resting on royal blue satin, looked like gold-wrapped Godiva chocolates.

"Here's my mom's raddled ribbon work," said Sandy, as she held a basket made of red, white, and blue ribbons woven in and out around a grid. The basket was stuffed with letters.

"Fan mail, partner. I have a letter from the President and from mayors of cities where nationals have been sponsored."

"Fantastic!" I spouted. "This room is deadly. It's a Ripley's Believe It or Not."

"I want to tell you, partner," said Sandy. "I love this stuff, but swimming as a soloist has been recycled too many times. I'm ready for something new. Together we can show the judges stunts they've never seen. From now on, it's double trouble for duets. We'll show 'em."

"Count me in," I agreed. "This is one splash party I can't afford to miss."

"Oh, it won't be a splash party when Mrs. Z gets fired up," warned Sandy. "Senior swimming is serious business."

Imitating Coach Zavitz, she made a stern face and hollered, "ONE MORE TIME. Remember that, Julie. It's the password used by the elite swimmers. You'll repeat a skill for Z even if you're dizzy."

Widening her fingers through her hair, she continued. "I hope you like mildewed hair and red eyes. We'll be in the wet stuff four nights a week plus workouts on Saturday and Sunday afternoons. Water will slosh around in your head." Looking hopefully at me, she asked, "Do you really want to join this flaky skin and water-logged body?"

"To tell the truth, I had some doubts," I admitted. "The idea of swimming as your partner swept me overboard. My mom said to go for it and my dad thinks the whole deal is awesome. Now I'm sold on the idea since you think I'm your ace partner." Thrusting my palms in a high-five gesture, I added, "Slap some fame on me, champ, and let's make waves together."

V

The Mighty Toad

Mrs. Z's elite class practice was soon to begin. I was a wreck.
My stomach quivered like a leaf on a limb in a windstorm.

"I'm a turtle compared to those girls," I complained to
Mom. "I can't match their skills. In ten minutes I'll make the
biggest belly flop of my life."

Mom's soft smile of sympathy should have helped, but
it didn't. Her words didn't sink in, either.

"By the look on your face, you haven't told yourself to
be happy," she said. "You're half-fish by now, Julie. Water is
your greatest delight."

Tears hung on my eyelids. I hated the feeling of being
the class blunderhead.

"I'm not sure I can keep up with Z and Sandy. My double ballet legs feel like lead pipes, I can't depend on hitting
vertical every time, and I'm still a sinker on my back. Really,
Mom, I'm a wet noodle half the time."

"Don't be upset before you give it your best," said
Mom. "Sandy will help you learn the fine points. Remember, Mrs. Z has confidence in your ability, so give yourself
time."

Beep, beep, sounded the horn from where Dad was
waiting. Sniffling my tears of doubt, I harnessed my pool
bag and stomped out of the house.

The drive to the pool was silent except for Dad's whistle. Having been a swimmer for the University of Michigan, he often whistled the varsity song.

"There's Sandy," he announced, hoping the sight of my partner would change my bad mood. "She's dancing on the sidewalk."

"She's great, Dad. I want to be just like her."

As I stepped out of the car, she hollered, "Hit the deck, Julie. A school of fish-eyed sea sprites is waiting inside."

"Waiting for what?" I asked, hustling to keep up with her.

"You'll see," she answered.

I found out the moment I entered the locker room. A ring of hand-clapping girls surrounded me. A chant, "Ju-lie, Ju-lie," broke out like a chorus of gospel singers. "ONE MORE TIME!" they hollered. My eyes popped open and probably sparkled like the Hope diamond. A finger-clicking routine followed, the neatest choreography ever. Eight counts of steady rhythm, then eight of syncopated beat. They mixed finger clicks with hand claps, tapped me on the shoulders and pinched my nose. Their legwork reminded me of the fast steps used in "River dancing." Simply amazing.

"Hold it, you guys," commanded Sandy. "We have an initiation gift for you, Julie." Sandy was holding a small box wrapped in water-wave paper. "Please open it now," she urged, settling a rock-heavy weight in my hands.

"It's so heavy," I said. "Is this an anchor, or what?" The weight forced my arms to unfold like the trunk of an elephant.

"Hurry," said Sandy. "Remember, Mrs. Z wants us in the water before the music begins."

Peeling away the wrappings, I saw a green warty toad of cast iron looking at me with bulging eyes.

"Welcome to the club of toads," hollered the girls.

Squeezing me like an octopus, Sandy cheered, "Now you're one of us. The toad is our mascot."

"Thanks, I think, for this toe cruncher," I said, a bit baffled at the ugly thing. "I, I, I'll use it as a door stop in my room."

My remark seemed to satisfy my new friends. They disappeared into the pool, leaving their newest toad behind. Hurriedly, I undressed and bunched my hair into a ponytail. Groaning with uncertainty, I said to myself, *Serious business, here I come.*

Ready or not, I stepped through the door, joined a group busy stretching muscles and testing flexibility. Mrs. Z paced the deck in her petite-size sneakers, wearing one of her fifteen bathing suits I had heard about. From the waist up, she could have won a swim suit contest. With her hair moussed stiff to hold a bouffant set and make-up the color of a ripe peach, she glowed like a Gerber's grown-up baby. Skintight leggings accented her petite derriere. A small microphone was attached to her suit and a stopwatch dangled from her neck. In less than ten minutes, the music started.

"Hit the water, Toads," she hollered. "Mix up your strokes to the music, four swimmers at a time. Thirty laps."

I flew from the deck out over the water, wanting to show my best racing dive. I felt completely in control until my eardrums vibrated from Mrs. Z's voice and talking whistle. She sounded like a cop on a corner directing traffic. Shrill stair-stepping tones from her whistle, along with hurry-up gestures of her arms, made me wonder if I was in the wrong lane or making illegal turns at the end of the pool.

"Kick, stretch, and move out," she bellowed. Her eyes seemed wild.

I stroked each lap in less and less time. Rumbling along like a sports car in overdrive, I shifted to the speediest gear. Flipping my turns, pushing off into a stretch, I did all the things ordered by Mrs. Z. When the music stopped, I was out of gas and my motor died.

"Line up on the lanes for overhead scoops," directed Mrs. Z. "Take off in waves of five."

Sandy saw me thump my arms on the deck in a feeble attempt to lift myself out of the way. Before I knew what was happening, she had hold of my limp body, dragging me on the slippery floor like a bag of wet towels.

"Don't bomb your first workout, Toad," she said, helping me to my feet. "Save some energy for scoops and sculls."

I gritted my teeth and slumped to a sagging pose. "I can't do overhead scoops even if I wanted to," I whispered to Sandy. "I'm too skinny. These legs sink the minute my arms go above my head."

"That's nothing new and I know the cure," said Sandy. "Do you like chocolate sundaes?"

"Who doesn't?" I responded. "What's the connection?"

With her face full of grins, Sandy answered. "Eat one every night after practice. Some fat on your bones will make you float like a cork. Here's the trick for now. When on your back, raise your fingers above the water at the end of each scoop. Your problem is common. We call it teeter-totter trouble. You're too light on one end and too heavy on the other."

"Starters," shouted Mrs. Z. "Take a layout with your hands holding the trough above your head."

The first wave of swimmers took their places, floating like lane markers awaiting the signal.

"Ready, set, go," came the command.

Five bodies launched like torpedoes heading for a target. Driven by sculling, hands flipping like fan blades, the swimmers stretched their legs and arms while skimming along the surface.

When my turn came, I tried to hold a floating position, but my legs kept sinking.

"Darn these lead weights," I moaned. Leaving the trough, I scooped and sculled overhead, trying exactly what Sandy had said. With some success I floundered along. Mrs. Z noticed my trouble. "This isn't a class for sinkers," she yelled."Get to the surface."

Finishing last made the ache in my throat want to escape. So I doused my head under and screamed until blood roared in my ears. No one could hear my scream. I was sure the water would reduce it to a mere sonar signal.

The air clearly carried Mrs. Zavitz's shout for team relays.

"Crawl, Back, Breast and Fly. In that order, please." Relays were music to my ears. Strokes were my best skills. At last, a chance to help my team win. Something inside my modest outside began running, laughing and jumping. Jockeying for a position in the line-up, I found myself the anchor swimmer on lane five.

"Come on, legs, get kicking," I commanded. At the whistle, five bodies hit the water like cracks of thunder. Sandy, swimming in lane four, set the pace. She could swim like lightning. Her crawl was awesome. The second wave of back strokers skimmed along like kayaks. Then came the bobbing breast strokers with powerful whip kicks. I waited my turn to fly. The last swimmers before me matched strokes like pom-pom girls. I had to open a lead if my team was to win.

"Finish fast," I ordered myself. Inhaling while shaking every muscle limp, I crouched for the takeoff. With a mighty shove, I sprang horizontally over the water until my vertebra seemed to separate. Like Dad had said, I had a wing span of an eagle. "Attack, Jacobs," I demanded.

The swimmers were screaming and Mrs. Z. was bending over the finish line. Down the pool we came shoulder to shoulder and arm to arm. With a whale of a kick-stretch, I touched first.

"Lane five is the winner," shouted Mrs. Zavitz.

Those words brought such surges of bliss, I felt wobbly. Sandy jumped in and steadied me.

"Good show!" she hollered, holding my arms in the air like they do in the boxing ring. "Our Mighty Toad!"

VI

Golden Goddesses

After eating a chocolate sundae, I had gone to my room to dream. As I stared at my bulgy-eyed door stop, my spirits soared like a puffy cloud.

"I'm climbing and going places," I said to Jude. "With Sandy as my partner, I have a chance to compete with the best."

Water gurgled in my aquarium as Jude darted upward, then turned in a circle. Maybe she felt my excitement.

I was one of about five hundred U.S. senior swimmers having a free weekend. The coaches of elite swimmers were in Chicago for convention. Mrs. Z was there, of course. At that meeting, the bids for national meets would be accepted. I was dying from anxiety pains. Most synchro qualifiers were going zany until they knew their travel schedule.

"Maybe New York," I said to Jude, "or California. It doesn't matter where, just so I get to go."

To keep from going nuts, I spent my free weekend studying the tree chart of power in our state government. I made a flag for Earth Day and collected from the Internet data on the Genome Project. Free days without swimming were really a bore.

The night Mrs. Z returned, not one Toad was absent from class. Everybody came early. The locker room pulsated with crazy choreography. At least five different tapes of music were playing at the same time. Dance steps and body gyrations took over, more moves than my mother had taught me. We were hopping kangaroos when Mrs. Z arrived. Standing in the doorway, she blew her whistle and motioned for us to join her. We all galloped into the pool and sat down in one corner of the deck. I was so excited, my body had trouble containing my shaking.

"Well, Toads," she began, "we will chalk up air miles this time."

"Honolulu," I whispered to Sandy, who, with rolling eyeballs, returned a million-dollar smile. Mesmerized with the Hawaiian thought, we waited for Mrs. Z's next juicy tidbit.

"The teams will be in Boston, the solos in Houston, and the duets, in Salt Lake City."

I squealed as high as the Rockies. It mixed with yips and yaps from the other girls. If Sandy had grown a tail, it would have been wagging.

Waving her arms to quiet us down, Mrs. Z hollered, "You sound like a kennel of puppies." When we settled down, she continued. "Flying to these meets will take more cash than our club can afford. We need money. I propose a couple of money-raising projects. If we all dive in, between Thanksgiving and Christmas, we could sell fruit cakes. I'd like the mothers to manage the cake sale. By phone, the merchants, the state government people, the mayor's office, and other industries should be encouraged to buy. If companies gave fruit cakes to their staff, we would have money enough to charter a plane," she shouted triumphantly. "I say, let's deliver a thousand cakes and make headlines with our millennium sale."

"Ready and able," shouted one toad.

"I have six aunts who will buy," voiced another.

"I'll swim the distance to Utah," I cheered.

"My second plan," continued Mrs. Z, "involves two for the price of one, if you know that expression. In February, we will stage a gala water show: involve the beginners and the juniors, too. Your show routines will go to nationals with a few modifications to comply with competitive rules."

"Sounds super," cheered Sandy, and we all joined in.

"Yah, super. When do we begin?"

"Here and now," answered Mrs. Z, rather curtly. "I'll need volunteers and plenty of committees. I mean, you may need to recruit the whole family."

Gathering her paper and pencil, she charged into her next plan.

"All right, girls. Let's talk water show. Pool your thoughts. Give me some ideas for a good theme."

One voice responded. "How about Lunar Labyrinth or Deep in Space?"

"I like Azure Asteroid or Wat'ry Galaxy," offered another.

Sandy hit a winner. "Oceans of Motions," she said with gusto.

The Toads all agreed and started to dig their minds for show biz numbers.

"You gals have great ideas," said Mrs. Z. "Your minds work in a brilliant fashion."

All the adjectives in the dictionary couldn't describe how my mind was working. Sorting out what just happened made me woozy. I had a champion for a partner. I'd be on stage at home in a show. I'd fly west to the Rockies and compete against mature elite girls. How could I do all that with teeter-trotter trouble and a bouncing eggbeater? What's more, my body was still juvenile. I needed fat, curves, and bosoms. If my hormones refused to kick in, in time, I'd be swallowing fruit cake with my ice cream from now 'til next summer.

Mrs. Z added more details. "From this group, I expect routines that are eye-catching as well as competitive. Use tonight's class time to select your number for the show. Let me approve the choices before you leave here searching for music."

Sandy and I found a seat in the balcony. We were quiet at first, sitting in the Thinker pose, chin in hands and elbows on our knees.

"Think 'til you ache," said Sandy. "A good theme is tough to decide. Let's begin with the alphabet. Say the first word that comes to your mind. Like A is for Aladdin or Athenian."

"Arabesque," I added.

"Try B's," said Sandy.

"Ballet or the Buck," was my reply.

"Give me a C," asked Sandy, beginning to sound like a cheerleader.

"Oh, that's easy. The can-can, the Charleston, and the Cha-cha-cha," I said, adding body language and some rhythm.

Sandy's face began to brighten as if in a spotlight.

"We'll be dancers!" she said explosively. "You know the moves, Julie. You're a natural."

"Which dance?" I asked. "There are millions." Sandy's answer was not what I expected.

"With Oceans of Motions as the show theme, the sky is the limit. We could be dancers from space, like daughters of the Jedi. How about that, partner? You want to make your debut with science fiction and all that stuff?"

My jaw dropped and I drew a complete blank. My bag of steps didn't include space dancing. I had tried Michael Jackson's moon walk, but failed.

"You can't be serious," I moaned, as strange and unidentified feelings targeted my body.

"Just kidding," said Sandy. "You're the pro. You know umpteen authentic steps. Just tell me what dance is classy, sharp, and unique."

"Take your pick," I answered. "I know scads of steps: American, European, Asian and Oriental."

Again, we were quiet while our minds explored the possibilities. I broke the silence. "My mom is terrific at Siamese. She can goose-neck like a pendulum and her arms bend like a swastika."

"Fantastic! I love it," shouted Sandy. "A built-in choreographer. Come on, partner. Let's tell Mrs. Z."

Coach Zavitz highly approved. Unloading a storehouse of helpful tips, she scribbled names I'd never heard before.

"Here is a list of CDs in the library that contain good music for your theme. 'Dance of the Siamese Children' comes to my mind. Music from *Scheherazade* and *Kismet*, though very old, are excellent compositions." Turning to me, she added, "I'll bet your mom can design a striking costume. Ask her, for me, please."

Sandy and I left the pool feeling as if we were on our way toward winning the biggest contest in our lives. Chanting, "Siamese, if you please," we faded out of the room.

"Okay, partner," said Sandy. "Hit the library tomorrow after school."

"Gotcha," I answered.

Dad was waiting for me in the parking lot. As I approached his car, for his benefit, I telegraphed my new routine. With each step, I did the goose-neck. He read my act perfectly and tooted the car horn in rhythm. Beep, b-beep-beep. Before taking a bow, I posed like the statue in Bangkok known as the many armed goddess.

I spilled the good news over and over to Dad. He hurried a little extra to get me home before I became hysterical.

Almost before the car had stopped, I was out and running. My giant steps thundered all the way to Mom's sewing room. Wearing a cheek-to-cheek smile, I hollered, "Mrs. Jacobs. May I introduce you to the golden goddess of Siam, who will appear next spring in Salt Lake City."

With a gasp of air, Mom rose from her chair. Spreading her arms, she snuggled me into a hug as tight as a clam.

"Siamese," she said, releasing me. "Won't that be splendiferous." Mom often coined her own words, especially when she was excited.

My tongue wagged with happiness. "I'm the luckiest girl in the world. Nothing can stop us now. Sandy is my partner, Mrs. Z is tops at coaching champions, and you, Mom, I hope, will be our professional costume designer and choreographer."

"Wait a minute, Julie. We're moving too fast. Let me learn this script before the curtain opens. Did I hear you say designer and choreographer?"

"Please, Mom. Say yes. Nobody around here has your know-how. Mrs. Z wants you to make the costumes. She knows how original and extraordinary your creations can be. A feather-weight suit is what she wants. Nothing heavy 'cause she expects us to walk on the water. Well, almost."

"I get the picture. You've stirred my imagination," said Mom. "Perhaps gold lamé spandex material is available. A collar of beads with fancy ribbon trim could supply the pizazz. Decorated turret hats would be striking."

Mom's ideas were flowing like a river and she was caught in the current.

"Z needs to see your sketches before you start sewing. The hats sound super for the water show, but not for competition."

"WATER SHOW! What water show?" Mom's voice moved up scale.

"Oceans of Motions," I explained. "It's one of Mrs. Zavitz's money raisers to help pay the air fares. The show will be in February, ahead of the national meets."

"That Mrs. Z is a dynamo," said Mom. "Her supply of energy could fill the Grand Canyon. So, you will debut with Sandy in the show and then bedazzle the judges in Utah."

"Exactly, Mom. Isn't that awesome?"

With a pencil in hand, she started drawing parts of our costume. I could tell her mind was buzzing with ideas.

So far, so good, I said to myself, but there were two more demands on her time; our choreography and the fruit cake sale. Should I tell her more and ask for help? I knew the answer. My parents had helped me get from the bathtub to a qualifying position in senior national competition. They wouldn't quit now. So, I kept going.

"Could we talk dance?" I asked, hopefully. "Sandy and I really need your help. We'd love to goose-neck to impress the judges." Mom's professional opinion diluted my eagerness.

"Just don't be carried away with a loosey-goosey neck movement. To eggbeater and goose-neck at the same time seems awkward. I'd concentrate on true Siamese: sharp angles that end in a stationary pose high above the water."

"You're right, Mom. That's a good tip, 'cause Z's half and half exercise is a killer. I'd die trying to wiggle my head and eggbeater fast enough to stand waist high. We could do it in our deck dance, right?"

"The fine points will come later," said Mom. "The music will dictate the choreography."

The next day, after school, I found Sandy in the audio wing of the library editing music. With earphones, a stop watch, and a pencil, she was listening, timing parts, and numbering beats.

"Super music," she whispered. "It's perfect." Handing

me her paper of notations, she asked, "Have you ever edited music?"

"Never," I answered, shaking my head.

Sandy made me dive right in. She clamped the earphones over my ears, saying, "Cut means a good place to splice in some different music. The beats are numbered in eight counts, and a section of music having a natural ending, is the slash mark. I'll listen to the other pieces that Mrs. Z suggested while you checkout the Siamese March."

Within seconds, the fun began. Crazy over what we were hearing, parts of our choreography began to take shape. There in the hush of the library, our pantomime of old Siam came alive. The air filled with flinging arms, flat-footed steps, and body contortions. Putnam Library was more like a stage for interpretive dancers.

The deepest of readers peeped around the door to watch our uninhibited gyrations. The lady at the front desk sensed some foul play. Moving in flight like a silent moth, she appeared at the scene of the disorder. In a frightening whisper, she said, "Girls, girls, You must stop this spectacle."

Sandy and I froze in a pose. Sandy spoke for me too. "We're sorry, Mrs. Lynch. We were carried away with the music. Our new swimming routine is going to be Siamese."

Mrs. Lynch was furious. "Siamese, Japanese, Burmese, or Chinese makes no difference. You better swim yourself out of this building in double time. WE LISTEN AND READ IN HERE."

Before being reduced to mini oil slicks by the lady's fiery eyes, we stuffed our high spirits, beats, and splices into an envelope and made a quick exit.

"Seems like we're always getting into trouble," I sobbed as I mounted my bike. "First the lifeguard and now the librarian. Am I the cause?"

"Heavens, no," answered Sandy. "We picked the wrong place to get excited over our music. No problem. Keep cool, partner." Wearing a satisfied grin, she added, "I have enough notes for Mrs. Z to make a tape recording, and for sure, we have oceans of motions. See you tonight at the pool." Off she went humming "March of the Siamese Children."

VII

Oceans of Motions

Small tornadoes of fine snow spiraled across the fields being pushed by a February wind. It was the day after Valentine's day, opening night of the water show.

Dad had gone to warm up the car before chauffeuring me to the pool. Completely dressed in costume, I was with Mom in front of the mirror. She was conducting a final examination of her dazzling creation. The gold lamé suit fit like skin. The collar of sequins and metallic braid draped my shoulders. A three-tiered hat, sparkling with jewels, sat securely over my beehive hairdo.

"It's perfect, Mom," I said, turning left and then right to catch my profile in the mirror. "Finally curves and round mounds. A fully female body," I cheered. "Sort of a miracle since last year. My boobs have arrived. Hooray! The teeter-totter trouble is over."

"Oh yes, Ms. Siam," responded Mom. "The female metamorphosis you've been hoping for has happened. You are a young lady with an hourglass figure and an inch of cleavage to prove you're a woman," exclaimed Mom, proudly.

"And you are a cool lady, a real genius. No one will ever guess my hat is made from the insides of a flour sifter and two tea strainers. Mission accomplished, Mom. It's light as a feather."

After stepping into my Aquarius sweat pants, I shoved my arms into a long winter coat. With a tape recorder in one hand and my duffle in the other, I was ready for Oceans of Motions.

"Break a leg and keep your nose pinched," jollied Mom, meaning give a great performance with my clips secure.

As I plodded down the walk in my cleat boots, Mom hollered, "You look more like a nomad than a Siamese goddess."

My overloaded duffle strained at the seams as I stuffed it between Dad and me. Of course, he noticed the fat thing. "You must have more in there than a certified plumber would carry," he teased.

"Just essentials," I chirped. "Mrs. Z said to come prepared. I have pins for my hair, nose cement, needles and thread, aspirin for aches, and granola bars. If my warty toad had been lighter, it would have come, too. Some girls toss in sleeping bags and bushels of stuffed animals."

"I haven't heard you grumble over practice, or sing the blues lately," said Dad. "So how's it going?"

"Mrs. Z says I'm nearly blooper free. Finally, I'm a floater. I know how to execute every single figure in the handbook. Sandy is happy. She thinks we'll be tough to beat at nationals."

"LOOK AT THIS!" shouted Dad, as we came into view of the pool. "Mrs. Z has gone star crazy."

All along the road, windsocks waved like giant squids. Two blue spotlights shone on an icy rotating model of the world. As it turned, thousands of sparkles shot outward from the sphere. Polka music filled the air as a sextet of "Czechoslovakian" dancers repeated, hop-step-together-step.

"Your coach is almost as great as Disney," exclaimed Dad. "What I've seen so far sure will sell tickets."

As the car stopped, a young guy opened my door.

"I'm supposed to help swimmers get to the locker room," he said. "Let me carry your duffle." Flinging it over his back, he looked like Santa. His eyes twinkled, his dimples were merry, his cheeks were like roses and his nose like a cherry. To mention his looks would have embarrassed him, so, I gasped and said, "I don't believe this. I feel like a celebrity."

Dad hollered something about sitting six rows up during the show, but this Santa fellow slammed the car door before Dad finished. My brain was sorting like a computer. I had seen this guy before, but where? As we walked toward the pool door, he announced, "You are a Golden Goddess. I can tell from your hat."

"Good observation," I answered, still dredging my mind for a clue about him.

"I've read the show program," he said. "Our names are listed together under 'Dance of the Siamese Goddesses.' "

"WHAT?" I squawked like a scared bird. "YOU ARE IN MY ROUTINE?"

"According to Mrs. Zavitz, I'm your prop," he answered. "I'm the golden Buddha in your spotlight."

"Golden! How do you manage that?" I asked.

"Your coach knows a heap about theatrical gimmicks. She gave me the formula. First, I cover my body with mineral oil and then rub gold powder into the oil. Presto, the golden Buddha. Because I'm a statue, I can't even blink. My eyes will be closed. I'll be sitting cross-legged on a platform right behind you during your deck dance. Mrs. Z also wants me to dive at halftime. Oh sorry, you call it intermission."

"I take it you dive before you turn gold," I said with a tad of tease.

"Absolutely. After our act, I'll be under the shower scrubbing gold for hours. I have two bottles of dishwashing detergent to do the job." He continued without a pause. "I dive for Country Day High. I'm a sophomore. My friend and I do comedy stuff we learned at diving camp. If you can, blow the locker room and come out to watch us ham it up."

As he opened the door to the building, we whisked into the warm hallway. He deposited my duffle, turned and with a pogo spring in his step, walked away saying, "See you at halftime."

I ran like a gazelle to the ticket booth and snatched a program. Sure enough, a Todd Webster was listed as the golden Buddha. His name didn't ring a bell, but his rosy face was as clear in my mind as a Kodak glossy print. *Who is that dude?* I pondered. *Maybe he worked in the ice cream store. I've stuffed down chocolate sundaes for months. I wonder if he remembers me? Probably not, 'cause I've changed into a woman.*

Anxious to check out this Buddha thing with Sandy, I headed for the makeup room.

"Siamese, if you please," announced the lady who had just finished Sandy's face. My partner glowed yellow beige from the waterproof tanning lotion on all her exposed parts. Seeing me, she arched her hand until her golden fingernails curved upward like the roof of a pagoda.

"How do I look?" she quipped, turning a three-sixty.

"Devastating!" I replied. Sandy's almond shaped eyes had been outlined almost to her temples. Her arched eyebrows were in coal-black pencil. My mom's three-tiered hat sat securely on her head like a steeple.

"Next," said the makeup artist, looking at me and pointing at the stool. "I need two goddesses exactly alike, so sit here, please, for my treatment."

Straddling the stool, I asked my anxious question of Sandy. "Did you know about the golden Buddha before tonight?"

"No, not exactly," answered Sandy, "but Mrs. Z re-

47

serves the right to add her finishing touches. Sounds neat. Who's the Buddha?"

"I think he was at the duet finals last year. My dad called him a bullfrog, I named him King Neptune. According to the show program, he is Todd Webster. He called me Aphrodite loud enough for a balcony of people to hear. I think I owe him one," I said, feeling impish. "Hit me with some prankish ideas, partner."

"With pleasure!" responded Sandy, who had a galloping love for good jokes. "Maybe we could make him sneeze when he's in the spotlight. I have some hair spray that tickles my nose."

"Keep going," I urged. "Love your quick-witted ideas."

"Plop a hair bow on his head just before the spotlight hits us. He wouldn't dare to move. We could borrow a bow from one of the girls in the Western Hoedown routine," said Sandy.

"Wait. I have it," I shouted, raising my hand like a second grader with the answer. The makeup lady jumped backward, anxious to hear my scheme. "If he's going to be one of us, he needs a toad. A bunch of the girls have toad Beanie Babies. Let's put a toad on the platform right in front of him."

Imagining the scene, made the makeup lady giggle. "You are finished," she said, shaking her head. "Go have your fun."

"Final call for the opening number," came a voice from the program coordinator. "Line up in the hall."

Within minutes, a parade of old Polynesia appeared. Young beginner synchro's dressed in floral sarongs, with leis over their shoulders and flowers in their hair, filed by the makeup room. Chubby girls carrying small canoe paddles, painted hot pink on one side and cool lavender on the other, wiggled the hula as they passed us. Next came a

48

dozen or so swimmers wearing black tank suits carrying small dark flutter boards decorated with brightly colored nylon flowers.

"Darling. Just adorable!" exclaimed Sandy. "I know we're to stay in this room 'til it's time to perform, but we can't miss seeing this number. It's done in black lighting, one of Mrs. Z's spectaculars. I heard she has a volcano on deck with lava flowing into the water. Come on, partner. Follow me.'"

Sandy took a route used only by the custodians. Moving quietly, we sneaked through halls and down into a narrow passageway under the pool where the motors hissed and the drains gurgled.

"There is an exit door down here that leads to some steps up to the pool deck, if I remember," said Sandy. "I went through here at the open house when this pool was built."

By now, I was feeling guilty and wanted to go back.

"Mrs. Zavitz will drown us if she finds out we came down here," I said.

"Don't panic. We can handle this," Sandy assured me.

At the far end of the bulging belly of the pool, a red exit sign burned.

"There's the door," said Sandy, hustling along the bowels of the tank. "Hope it's unlocked." Carefully turning the knob, she released the latch.

"Lucky," she whispered excitedly, "but, we can't let this basement light spoil the black lighting or we'll be discovered."

"Here's a switch," I said, pointing to the wall.

"Don't touch it," ordered Sandy. "It could be the light in the pool stairwell."

"Let's go back," I coaxed.

"No. I have a plan. I'll flick the switch like a flash camera. If the basement goes black, we have it made."

Blink went the lights overhead. The basement was a deep black hole. Like caterpillars, we inched through the crack in the door and climbed the stairs on our hands and knees until our eyes adjusted to the fluorescent scene. There in the ink black waves, a symphony of colors moved like pieces in a giant kaleidoscope. At the deck edge, a row of saronged swimmers sat paddling to a rippling guitar. The down stroke glowed pink and the recovery, lavender.

"It even smells good," I whispered, sniffing the air.

"Mrs. Z's sets are always colossal and jazzed up. Would you believe atomizers are attached to the flutter boards? One squeeze and the pool is a perfumery," said Sandy, quietly.

"WOW! I thought Mrs. Zavitz loved the competitive athletic side of synchronized swimming," I whispered. "Didn't she say to think sport, not stage?"

In a low voice, Sandy answered. "She loves both. When she went to college, synchro was popular among the artsy people. I've seen her collection of Esther Williams movies. Fountains came up from the bottom of the pool, swimmers swung over the water on a trapeze, and floating patterns opened and closed like giant water lilies. Mrs. Z told me the real challenge is the sport. Props and scenery are not allowed. Swimmers can't walk on the bottom of the pool 'cause they would be disqualified."

"I remember," I said. "The show goes on for the money and fun, but the money goes out for the sport."

"Right, partner," agreed Sandy. "The income from Oceans of Motions will fly us to Salt Lake City for the nationals."

"Don't remind me," I pleaded. "I get jittery when I think about nationals."

As the black lighting faded, an octave of guitar harmony soared upward from behind the volcano. A mellow conch shell sounded as the last waves spilled into the trough. Closing the liquid stage from the audience, a curtain of water spewed upward and each droplet fell in a mist over the pool. The swimmers made their exit under the glistening canopy.

"Move out and stay low," ordered Sandy, hunching her back. To escape from being seen, like sinking vessels, we submerged down the stairs.

As Sandy opened the door, a monstrous shadow darkened half of the walls in the basement.

"We left this room in a total blackout," I announced in full voice.

"Sh-sh-h-h. Someone is down here," whispered Sandy, peeping around a pipe with a swollen elbow. "It's the custodian. He's taking a nap."

Prowling along, we stepped as softly as kittens on cotton. Slithering through the upper hall door, we sealed out the man and his gurgling snore.

"Score ten for that maneuver," cheered Sandy. "Now let's deck our routine."

The main hallway was a river of music. The practice rooms were tributaries of sound. From one came the skirl of bagpipes, from another pulsations of dervish drums, and the repetitive treble notes of the square dance fiddle sent me into a shuffle. I backed into the makeup room clapping and stepping to the music. Bent over with my hips leading, I continued until, in the corner of my eye, I saw a barefooted, barelegged and barechested young male figure. Afraid to look up at him, I froze on one leg like a water bird. He bent over forcing our eyes to meet.

"How-de-do-de!" he drawled, raising his eyebrows. "Are you the goddess I met at the car, or Fanny Farmer?"

Flooding with blush, I straightened and released the first thing I could think of.

"Aren't you out of your corral? This is filly territory."

In a fake Texas drawl, he answered, "I came for oil and gold dust, Ma'am." Hanging his thumbs from his swim trunks, he continued, "This is where Mrs. Zavitz said I would strike it rich. My makeup is in here."

I quick-stepped to the table of supplies and palmed a jar of gold powder and a plastic bottle of mineral oil. Handing him the items, I quipped, "Pay dirt, mister." With a nervous choke in my throat, I introduced Sandy.

"Todd, meet my partner, Sandy Jenkins. Sandy, this is Todd Webster, our Buddha."

"Hi, Todd," responded Sandy. "So you're Mrs. Z's gold dust statue who can't see or move. Sounds weird, but you'll probably steal the show."

"Doubtful," he replied. "You two are the big stars with top billing."

"I'm not a star yet," I said crisply. "I'm Sandy's new partner. Mrs. Z put us together right after the duet nationals."

Todd looked at me as if admiring the chassis of his first set of wheels. "WOW! You sure have changed since then," he exclaimed. "In this makeup, you're a chiller."

I hissed like a frightened kitty but managed to smile pleasingly, 'cause I felt a tinge of fancy for him.

"I'd like to see you after the show," he said, "but gold doesn't wash off easily. I'll be scrubbing for hours."

His words, after the show, tantalized my ears. I whipped a reply. "Well then, pop in tomorrow night before the show. I'll be right here."

"Cool, real cool," he agreed. Leaving the room, he executed a slam dunk at the top of the door.

"Nice guy, partner," said Sandy. "Let's start concentrating on our routine before you soar off on a cloud."

Over and over again, a total of seven times, we walked through our choreography. Seven was Mrs. Z's number. Way back in her training, she learned that memory became habit after repeating an exercise seven times.

"Goddesses next," came the announcement from a head that poked through the open door.

"Quick, it's countdown," ordered Sandy. "Tighten your hat, stuff a pair of nose clips under your leg elastic. Where's the nose cement? Get the toad for Buddha." Sandy was acting like a big sister ordering me around.

"No toad tricks," I answered. "I've lost my nerve. Todd is too nice a guy and Mrs. Zavitz might throw a fit."

"You're probably right. Here, catch," said Sandy, tossing a granola bar. "Chow down, partner. We have at least five minutes before we're on."

Out of the practice room, we pranced along like young fillies who had just eaten oats instead of granola bars.

"My ears are popping when I swallow!" I groaned.

"That's proof your nose clips are tight," answered Sandy.

Once inside the pool room, we moved behind the screen of the volcano. A narrow spotlight focused on the announcer seated inside the model of a world globe. While the audience watched and listened to his rich voice, we took our places in front of Buddha.

"Go for it," he whispered. My heart skipped a beat.

"Ladies and gentlemen," said the master of ceremonies, "from Southeast Asia come the goddesses of Siam, to move majestically across our liquid stage. Performing as one, in a state of complete happiness, they represent harmony in the sea of life."

At first, the spotlights were blinding. I was behind

Sandy, in part of her shadow. From the audience's view, Sandy had four arms. When the music began, two arms raised as two arms lowered. Accenting angular poses, we slowly moved apart until Buddha was in the light. The audience made oohs and aahs, probably because his gold shimmered flicks of fire. At a musical high point, Sandy and I stepped out into space and knifed downward into the water. At nine feet deep, it was murky turquoise, but I saw my partner smile. Planting our feet on the bottom, we pushed upward. Like a rocket, we shot to the surface and continued to climb until hip high. Twisting a 360 at our height and twisting another as we descended, gave the routine a spectacular beginning. Our choreography had all the requirements for national competition: leg splits, pivots, walkovers, and unique originals. Before our routine reached the halfway point, the audience joined in. Fans hollered, "Go for the gold." Others clapped to our music. I psyched up. My mind kept saying, *climb waist-high, scull for your life, and one more time.* Our five-minute routine was the happiest time of my life. When it was over, I had energy to spare. My final pose was waist high and steady. I was kicking the eggbeater double time.

Flowers splashed onto the water. Sandy caught a nosegay of golden roses. I swept up a bouquet, shouting, "Thank you, everybody. Thank you."

Cheers continued even after the lights faded.

"Great performance," said Todd, trying to keep up with us as we made a fast exit. "I didn't want to miss the main attraction, so Buddha opened his eyes after you two jumped in. You were flawless. How can you be so together?"

"We signal under water," answered Sandy.

"We're like talking porpoises," I added. "Believe it or not, Mrs. Z thinks our synchronization will pull a ten from the judges in Utah. Wow! Will that be something. I've never had a ten."

"Just remember, partner," said Sandy. "You don't yell 'thank you' to the national judges."

"Got it, champ," I agreed. "This girl will just smile."

Leaving wet footprints in the hall, we hurried to the makeup room. Looking at Todd, who was greasy gold, I asked, "Did your big toe cramp while sitting like a pretzel?"

"What an aching thought," he answered, "but that would never happen. I stretch the heck out of my feet and ankles before diving."

"You were a deadly Buddha," I said, not realizing the corny pun. "Thanks for the neat prop."

His next remark was really absurd. "How about using me at nationals? We could start a new trend."

"No way," I shouted. "Not a chance. At nationals, it's all sport. Water show stuff is taboo. Your greasy get-up would disqualify us."

"Seriously, Julie," he said, looking me in the eyes, "good luck in Utah. I think you are terrific, a cool ten." From his feet, rivulets of gold and oil were forming on the floor.

"I better go scrub. See you later," he said.

"Okay," I answered, feeling happy about the duet and my relationship with Todd.

Sandy and I were show stoppers for the next evening's performance. We decided to change our opening choreography from a rocket double twist to a stop dive twist. We startled the fans, probably because they had never seen swimmers dive into nine feet of water and stop in a vertical before their feet disappeared.

The next day's newspaper featured us on the front page of the sports section. It read, "Jacobs and Jenkins prospect for gold in Utah."

"You better believe it."

VIII

Spring Training

Months of Mrs. Z's spring training had me over my head in serious business. It seemed as if she was preparing my body for a boxing title instead of a synchro honor. Twice a week I'd zip over to a health club for weight lifting and treadmill workouts. A therapist had shown me how to count and time my pulse and keep a record of it. For some reason, an expert in physics had determined my specific gravity.

"I just want a body like yours," I said to Sandy. "What's all this science?"

Sandy cued me in on what was happening.

"Z keeps a record of our physical development. She's writing a book and conducting a research project for the university. She has a list of tests and measurements used for peaking her athletes. Believe me, she'll try every one of them before she's through. Now that you can float, I predict she will stop the chocolate sundae routine."

"Too bad," I groaned. "That part was super." Standing as tall as the Statue of Liberty, I took a deep breath and said, "At the pace I've been training, I'll be ready to climb the Rockies once I get there."

Sandy's eyes lit up with that idea. Mountain climbing presented an exciting adventure. Anything Sandy could possibly achieve, she faced with enthusiasm. I was so lucky to have a partner who would never cheat, make excuses, or fall behind when the doing became rough.

"The really tough training is coming next," said Sandy. "Z hands out weighted bands for our wrists and ankles. We'll be sculling meter miles and kicking for twenty minutes wrapped in lead. Get ready for aching arms and jumpy thighs."

"Z must believe the athlete's golden rule, no gain without pain," I said.

"Everybody knows Mrs. Zavitz is a perfectionist. She delivers champions. I hold the U.S. crown because of her coaching," said Sandy, giving credit to the woman she admired.

"Are you on Z's diet?" she asked.

"Yep," I answered. "Gluey oatmeal for breakfast, a sandwich with raw veggies and Gatorade at noon, and, soup at night before practice. Soup sloshes in my stomach more than water rumbles in my ears. On the night we don't swim, I stuff in the works. Pizza and Big Macs go down with pleasure."

"Four more months to go and then the big finale," said Sandy, sounding jubilant as she slithered into the water. "Let's do our sculling in tandem. Cradle your feet under my head, partner. Twenty laps."

In a flat back layout, we connected in a chain, my feet to her head. Moving up and down the pool like an engine connected to a freight car, we completed the drill. As we rested at the shallow end, I asked Sandy who invented sculling? In a matter-of-fact voice, she supplied the info as if having read the answer in the encyclopedia.

"Finning came first because fish used that technique, but finning didn't support weight. Then some genius watched a hummingbird. Its wing movement could lift, lower, and drive forward or backward. Similar to its wings in air, a human, using his hands and forearms in the water, produce a smooth control of weight and drive. Presto, a kind of aqua-gymnastics was born. Sculling became a synchro's trademark."

Mrs. Z blew a three-whistle command.

"Underwater sprints are next," she announced. "Two lengths for now, but before nationals, double the distance."

I softly complained to Sandy, "I can scull and kick laps, but holding my breath makes me light headed."

"Think fish, partner. Ignore your desire to breathe," said Sandy, giving me a pain of punishment expression.

I inhaled until I felt like a balloon. Squatting on my heels with two or more feet of water above my head, I pushed off to cruise along the bottom of the pool. One lap made me dizzy. Two laps were disastrous. Mrs. Z was so busy hollering one more time, I was sure she didn't see me unload my soup in the trough. WRONG! She had her eagle eyes on every underwater body. I was no exception.

"Deck it, Julie," she hollered. "Forget the fish trips. Take a break. Go watch the video. Run the film in slow motion."

I did as she said. Wrapping in a towel like a mummy, I headed for a dark closest where a projector was ready to roll. In less than a minute, I was watching the incredible skill of the Pan American Games champion. Sandy walked in just as I said, "This gal is flawless. I can't execute like that. Mrs. Z is dreaming if she thinks I can imitate these moves."

"Oh yes, you can and you will at nationals," assured Sandy. "You look almost that good now. You've passed the bone age and lost the toothpick figure. You know all the do's and don'ts. What's left is the problem all elite athletes face, to always be excellent."

Mrs. Z popped her head in the door, saying, "It's figure

critique time. Come, let me see your figures for Utah. Sandy, you go first."

Sandy was cool and confident. Her body was limber, her legs educated, and every move she made looked easy.

"Bravo," praised Mrs. Z as Sandy perfectly executed a Sub-Crane. "Your moves are effortless and your line is plumb."

For a second the word "plumb" made my eyeballs search for the meaning, but the search was hopeless. Everything inside my skin was jiggling with jitters knowing I was next. I tried to appear eager, but my courage had escaped. My smile was weak and so were my legs. Sandy guessed how I was feeling.

"Relax, partner, and treat us with those gorgeous wading-bird legs," she said, with a grin that deepened the dimples in her cheeks.

"Your turn, Julie," said Mrs. Z. "Do a Flamingo, spinning three-sixty."

I assumed a back layout and slowly moved my legs to vertical. My sculling should have made quiet whirlpools, but I could hear the water slurp. With puffed cheeks, I pressed downward, opening until my head was under my hips. My balance was like a ship about to capsize, so the spin wobbled all the way down. I hated to come to the surface. Mrs. Z would throw a book of corrections at me.

"ONE MORE TIME!" she shouted. "Get rid of that balloon face. Don't telegraph to the judges the difficulty of that figure. Hit vertical, not a five-degree tilt. Grunt or swallow, but don't die to breath."

Hearing all that, I exploded with an uncivilized scream of terror and words that described my performance.

"I stink, I sink, I wobble. I'm a slimy wet noodle."

"One more time," repeated Mrs. Z calmly.

One more time became six more times before she finished with me. Dizzy as a drunken loon, I held my head in the trough.

"Sorry, Julie," she said. "You'll be just fine as soon as you become a water mammal. Right now, your problem is an oxygen deficit."

I snorted with contempt at what sounded worse than pneumonia. At least she didn't call me an airhead, which would have exactly described my condition.

"We've all had an overdose of practice for tonight," said Coach Zavitz. "Come, sit down, and listen a minute."

Flopping my body onto the tile, I sprawled like a tired dog. Hoping to put some starch into my limp-looking anatomy, Mrs. Z gave a pep talk.

"You two will make us proud. I'm pleased with your progress. The goddess routine is brilliant. Your figures are a challenge, but they can be polished in the weeks ahead. You are not at the peak of your training, but climbing." With a confident smile, she added, "Gold is my favorite color, so dive a little deeper. Keep at it, girls. Earn those nuggets."

She said what she meant, but I had to think about it. Could I become a champion with that invisible monster, an oxygen deficit, hanging around my neck, and, when on earth would I have the breath control of a water mammal?

When Mrs. Z had gone to help other swimmers, I moaned to Sandy. "I hope she's right 'cause so far I'm terrible. Suppose I get dizzy in Utah?"

"You won't," answered Sandy. "Workouts at home are lots worse than competition. Z's 'one more time' business is a dose of the dizzies. At nationals, you'll coast through figures. Trust me, partner. I've been there and done that. Think elite, 'cause that's what you are, Toad."

I said almost nothing to Dad as we drove home. My lack of confidence was pulling me under, and I was sure good luck had washed down the drain. Going directly to the kitchen, I found Mom making my favorite after-swimming snack: toast with melted butter, sprinkled with sugar and cinnamon, floating in a pool of warm milk. I couldn't eat a thing. The sight of food was gagging. As the toast soaked up the liquid, I poured my sad story to Mom.

"If I could just swim the routine in Utah and let Sandy do the figures, I'd be so happy. Sandy's stunts are super, but mine are awful. I was sick to my stomach after swimming the underwater laps and dizzy after a few spins. What if that happens at nationals? I can't say, 'Excuse me, judges. I'm going to throw up.'" Pounding the table as if it were the face of defeat, I kept grumbling.

"There's no chance to goof without a judge noticing. One little toe-off point reduces the score. I can't let Sandy down."

"Are you borrowing trouble or is Mrs. Zavitz concerned, too?" asked Mom.

"Mrs. Z is always upbeat," I answered. "Her rockets have already ignited. She thinks her top duet is ready for landing on the salt flats."

"Well then," stated Mom, "if your coach is satisfied, you shouldn't worry. Here's a morsel of philosophy to remember. Too many folks go through life running from something that isn't chasing them. Don't let fear defeat you. Your dizziness was not alarming to your coach because she has seen it happen before. Frankly, I think you need a break. For months you have lived in the water. No parties, no movies, and no fun. You can't take time to mosey home from school with a gang of girls, and I doubt if you've smiled at a boy since the water show."

"But, Mom," I wailed, "I love synchro. I just need more training. My body isn't ready yet. I have to perform with less oxygen. I'm supposed to grunt or swallow in place of breathing. Mrs. Z says I'll be fine when I become a water mammal."

"A WHAT?" screeched Mom. "Mrs. Z expects you to be as comfortable in the water as a hippo?! Preposterous! I think her serious business has gone too far. A water mammal. That's absurd." Mom kept sputtering like a pressure cooker.

"Attempting to enter this meet without confidence is hopeless. I'll discuss this with your father. He's an ex-athlete. He will dive to the bottom of this problem and come up with the answer."

I headed for my room muttering, "Jacobs. This mess is a dizzy-doozy."

Out of my sweat suit and into my PJs, I raised the bed covers and plunged under the sheet, wanting to hide from my irksome problem. Only Jay and Jude heard me repeat, "Think positively, think positively, think poz-z-z."

Daylight of the next morning brought shafts of raspberry red across my room. I stepped out of my cocoon wrappings with an appetite big enough to devour three bowls of oatmeal. Dad was dressed and waiting for me at the kitchen table.

"Good morning, Ms. Siam," he said, cheerfully. "We haven't talked much lately. What's the latest ripple at the pool?"

"Mom told you my problem, didn't she?"

"Oh, yes," he said. "A rather complete description."

"It's that 'one more time' business of Mrs. Z's," I complained. "I was nervous. Six times I executed a Flamingo spinning three-sixty. My brain turned balmy. I was a failure."

"Did Mrs. Z explain your problem?" asked Dad.

"Sort of," I said. "She thinks I'll be fine after I change to a water mammal."

"A very ingenious thought," said Dad. "This sounds like a whale of a story. You mean Mom and I will soon be living with an amphibian?"

"It's not funny, Dad. I can't be an airhead at nationals."

"Well, of course not." said Dad. "But tell me, has Sandy ever experienced this problem of dizziness?" he asked.

"I doubt it. She said Z's training was worse than competition."

Dad's face brightened and he smoothed my turbulent thoughts.

"Your coach knows what's happening. She doesn't operate by trial and error. She's equipped with the latest training methods. Her conditioning program is based on science. Should you continue to be dizzy, she will measure your lung capacity and know more about your athletic abilities. Trust her, Julie. If you have a bud of talent, Z will make it flower."

Standing erect, Dad spoke decisively.

"Jitters. You have the pre-meet jitters. That's all and it is not serious."

IX
Flight 711

Months of Mrs. Z's training were behind me. The oxygen deficit had been conquered and I had waded through a year of serious training.

"I'm flying away tomorrow," I cheered for Mom's benefit. Ignoring me, she kept stitching her surprise going-away presents. On the table lay my new gold lamé suit and a fantabulous finial for my head. The finial was a metallic band studded with cut jewels. The band when wrapped around a chignon anchored with my hair, would sparkle like a diamond tiara. That much pizazz had been approved by Mrs. Z.

"In Utah I'm going to be flawless," I told Mom. "The dizzies are dead and I can spin on my head. No one, I mean no one can call me a wet noodle 'cause my vertical has a perfect six o'clock line.

"I heard that," said Dad, walking into Mom's sewing room. "Confidence is the springboard to success. From it, you can hurdle most of life's obstacles. Sounds like you are ready to give your best in Utah."

"Right, Dad. I really hope for gold around my neck, but silver or bronze will feel just as good. I just want to do my best."

Smiling with pride, Mom displayed her gifts.

"This is your good-luck tag along mascot, complete and

64

ready to head west." She handed me a soft stuffed, fat-faced toad with a green back and tan belly. The creature was squashy and limp, the wet noodle type. I stood it on its head and stretched its legs. The boneless mascot smiled at me, then collapsed in a heap. It needed some synchro tips, so I tried to sound like Sandy.

"This won't be a splash party, Toad. Think sport, 'cause you're headed for serious business."

Mom, laughing at my foolishness, handed me another toad exactly like mine.

"This one is for Sandy," she said. I squealed with delight while cuddling its velvet body.

"These are adorable beanies. Sandy will love 'em." I perched the toads side by side on the table. They smiled at each other just like Sandy and I do before we perform.

"For sure, Mom," I said. "When the goddesses are announced at the Deseret pool and make a grand entrance, these toads will be sitting right on deck."

"There is more," said Mom, handing me a tote bag with the letters MAC appliqued to its front. "This is a carry-all to use when going from hotel to the pool. The pockets seal shut with velcro strips. The tote is water repellent and strong enough to hold your tape recorder. Your name label is ironed on, inside."

"Sounds perfect, Mom. *Merci beaucoup!* Tell me. What's the long word you use when something is wonderful? It came from an old movie."

"Supercalafabulistic," answered Mom, "but don't ask me to spell it."

"Nor I," said Dad. "I'm better with numbers. In fact, Julie, at twelve hundred hours, you must be in full travel uniform and ready to depart for the airport."

"That is exactly noon tomorrow," I cheered as pricks of

65

excitement began to torment my insides. "Bon voyage," I shouted and headed for my room to pack.

Jokingly, Dad hollered, "Don't attempt to load your aquarium. You will be in Utah for only three days."

I had made a list of things to take along, so stuffing my case was easy. The duffle swallowed baby oil, pins for my hair, Band-aids, M&M's, a crossword puzzle, photos of Jake and Jude, six pairs of nose clips, and finally my new toad.

"In you go, boneless," I said, chucking the mascot into a tiny space. "From now on, your name is One More Time." From its cramped position, a cute smile beamed at me.

"Okay, lovable. You are a charmer. I like your attitude. With practice you'll leap into next year's water show and be the star."

Having fun with One More Time ended when a noisy car arrived outside my house. It was loaded with kids shouting and a guy who played with the horn. From my window, I saw arms waving and faces looking. The car screeched to a stop, then jumped forward, several times as if dancing the Cha-cha-cha.

From that moment on, it was popular night for me. My home became a telephone connection center. Neighbors phoned to wish me good luck and I'll bet sixty Aquarius swimmers dialed my number. While I was in the shower, Mrs. Z's golden Buddha called and left a message.

"Your bullfrog fan," announced Dad, "wants to see you at the airport. I think he's croaking again to attract your attention."

My imagination flared. What super plan did Todd possess this time? What washed him off his lily pad? Maybe he was shocked by my homely picture in the newspaper announcing our meet in Utah.

"Did you give him my flight number, Dad?"

"No," answered Dad, with a tone of authority. "Focus

west, Julie. Forget Buddha for now. Prospect for gold, not boys."

When I climbed into bed, Jake and Jude were swimming their routine. Free and flowing, twisting and turning, their tail flips were effortless, so I gave them a ten.

For what seemed like hours, I wiggled and squirmed, lay pinching my lips and blowing hair off my forehead. Finally, after pounding the bed pillow, I felt my body relax.

It was late the next morning before I awakened to hear the water bubbling in the aquarium. Poor Jake and Jude never did go to sleep.

From the head of the stairs, Mom announced, "When you are dressed in your new travel outfit, I want to take pictures."

"She wants more," I said to my pets. "Would you believe her collection of photos fill a three-drawer chest? Every outfit she has made for me can be found in a picture."

I wiggled into a white tank top trimmed in turquoise, then stepped into a short turquoise skirt. A jacket of the same color identified my swim club. Mom had monogrammed its pocket with the letters M.A.C. White sandals with soft soles cushioned my feet. Instead of wearing my usual noseclip necklace, I hung my artsy gold ornament around my neck, a see-through dewdrop, with a swimmer inside posing in a flamingo bent-knee position. A local jeweler had made the charm from my pencil sketch.

I loved my mirror image. Wiggling with complete satisfaction, I shouted, "It's exactly what Sandy and I wanted. A teenager's sensation. You did it, Mom."

Sandy and her parents arrived just as the hands on the clock pointed to twelve. We all gathered in the yard. Hugs all around magically whisked me up in a cloud of affection. Mrs. Jenkins's friendliness flavored our flight with true happiness.

"I'm so glad," she said, "that Sandy is your partner. It's been a pleasure to watch you girls develop. You both are terrific athletes, and, in the water, look like identical twins."

Before I could say a word about Sandy, Dad hollered, "Pictures everyone. Get together. Nature's spotlight is shining."

We took turns with the camera, photographing combinations of people. Just as Dad ran out of film, a golden yellow convertible, escorted by a policeman on a motorcycle, turned into our drive.

"Surprise," shouted Dad. "Your chariot has arrived."

"A golden carriage!" exclaimed Mr. Jenkins. "You girls get to ride in deluxe style to the airport in this sporty model, a classy chassis from Detroit."

Dad shared his happy feelings while loading our duffles.

"This sendoff is rare. Our daughters are heading for the national championships. We're lucky parents to have such talent in our families." He patted the shiny yellow bumper and smoothed his hand over the leather upholstery. I felt as if I should invite him to ride along. Like a proud father, he shouted, "It's all yours, girls. Hop in."

Sandy and I climbed into our chariot. The top was open to the air, so we perched on the roof-line like two blue jays on a limb. Mom kept urging Dad to take more pictures. She didn't notice he was out of film, but she did realize our departure was happening fast.

"I'll be watching you on television," she hollered as we rolled down the drive.

"Is this a daydream, or for real?" I asked Sandy.

"I don't know yet, but I sure feel like the first woman president heading for the White House after my inauguration."

Frantically waving at our parents and everybody else

in the neighborhood, we realized our sendoff had been well planned.

As we passed the swimming pool, a bunch of kids cheered, "Go for gold." When we cruised through town, folks waved flags, tossed kisses, and held their thumbs in the air.

"What a neat surprise," I cheered. "Our dad's well-kept secret worked. I didn't have the foggiest idea about this scheme." We pinched and punched each other to be sure we were alive.

"I'm recording this trip in the diary of my mind," said Sandy, "and leaving a page for what's coming next. Mrs. Z told me, in Utah there will be a parade down streets as wide as a football field."

As we entered the outskirts of town, my thoughts, like Cupid's arrow, shot to the moment when I would see Todd and find out what he was up to. Maybe for some crazy reason, he was flying west.

"Guess who's at the airport?" I asked Sandy, happily. "Probably the whole swim club," she said blithely.

"Todd will be there. He called me last night and left the message." Sandy shook her head and gave me a no-no look of warning.

"Be careful, partner. Mrs. Z will want us to stay with her and board the plane together. Remember, you are now one of her prized protégés. She says boys are a distraction and interfere with an athlete's concentration. I hope Todd doesn't cause Mrs. Z to see red."

"Glad you told me, partner. I don't want to cause a bad time for anyone. I'll just wave when I see him."

Once at the airport, a riot of fun met us face to face. Aquarius club members were waiting inside the terminal beyond the revolving doors. In two lines, they formed an aisle for Sandy and me.

"Give 'em five," cheered Sandy, as we bounced along the aisle in a half-jogging step like professional basketball players. Cascades of giggles were all around us. Slapping the hands of swimmers we had not seen since the water show, we turned on smiles as bright as spotlights. Those novice and junior athletes were dreaming elite. They just needed a few years of sculling, walking on the water, and grunting like a water mammal to qualify for top competition.

At the end of the aisle, a motorized cart was waiting with Mrs. Z on board giving us directions.

"Pile in, girls. We're going directly to the gate. Your luggage will be checked by my agent."

With our beeper signal clearing the way, we opened a path. I scanned the crowd for Todd, but he was missing, probably smothered in the flow of travelers. Then, in the distance I heard running steps, heavy steps, and a voice saying, "Excuse me, excuse me." It was Buddha on the fast-track walkway, taking giant steps toward me. Before I could blink, he was running alongside of our cart. Squeezing a tiny gift into my hand, he said, breathlessly, "Open it just before you swim."

We sped away through the crowd as he stood waving. I stretched my arm above my head and sharply bent my wrist. He must have seen my flat hand twisting to the left and then to the right like a periscope. My boy-girl moment met with coach Z's approval, 'cause she winked at me from a smile of delight. I held Todd's gift of friendship in the palm of my hand until my fingertips numbed. Floating along in a sea of happiness, I was catching that awesome feeling called puppy love. I wanted to leap, do jetés, and pirouettes right there in the stream of travelers.

"Steady, partner," said Sandy. "Todd sure is the king of

surprises. I bet he will call you just before we swim. His timing is flawless."

Once on board the plane, Sandy took the window seat and I sat next to her in a row of three seats. Mrs. Zavitz sat across the aisle from us. As a look alike trio, we noticed people kept staring at our uniforms. Mrs. Z was wearing a white blazer with a turquoise blouse and skirt. Her pocket was monogrammed "USSS Official." Folks could only guess what those initials stood for. I heard one woman say we probably were part of a sailing team. Little did she know. With Todd's gift in my hand, I was sailing in pink punch paradise.

"I'm not waiting to open this gift," I said to Sandy, untying the ribbon. "Let's take a sneaky peek."

Sandy gave me that no-no look again.

"Don't do it, toad. What's in that box could be a lifesaver for us. I'm always nervous before I compete. We'll need something to keep us from gnawing our nails. Stuff it away 'til the big moment."

The plane was nearly full except for the aisle seat next to me. Seconds before pulling away from the gate, a broadchested guy with sorrel red hair headed toward me. Wearing a green-and-white jacket with a spartan shield, he was easy to identify as a student from Michigan State University. Stuffing his duffle above my head, he said, "Thanks for holding my seat." After giving us a once-over inspection, he lowered his big frame, squeezing his muscles against me. I froze in silence, but Sandy spoke with sudden boldness. "Glad you made it, Sparty. Now we can go."

His eyes shuttled from Sandy to me and back to Sandy like a sleuth searching for clues. "Am I seeing double or are you two the Wrigley Chewing Gum twins? This must be a Doublemint commercial. Where's the camera?"

Sandy supplied the answer. "We're from the Michigan

Aquarius club. We are sync swimmers on our way to the U.S. championships."

"Wait a minute," said the Spartan guy. "I must be talking to elite athletes. I've seen sync on TV. The stunts you do in the water are unbelievable." Riveting his eyes on Sandy, he continued, "You called me Sparty. Do you go to MSU?"

"No," answered Sandy with easy tact. "I've given demonstrations at your intramural pool."

"Ya know," said the Spartan. "I thought only ducks could tip up on their heads until I saw a sync do it. Maybe I should go see this phenomenal water-bird competition."

"Do it," urged Sandy. "Come to the Deseret pool on Saturday for the finals."

"By the way, I'm Jerry Chadwick. Who are you two?"

"Sandy and Julie," I blurted. "Jenkins and Jacobs, the goddesses of Siam."

"The what?" asked Jerry.

Sandy rescued me from that dumb remark. "Julie is saying the next time you see us, we'll be in gold lamé costumes with our faces painted. Our duet is a Siamese routine."

"I get it," said Jerry. "Your free exercise is to a theme like the figure skaters."

Over the roar of the engines, hours passed in conversation. It seemed like we learned more about Utah than we knew about synchro. Jerry told us the fun places to see. After he described the Raging Water Amusement Park, with nineteen roller-coaster water slides, my stomach was fizzing. Bubbles rose up and burst inside my throat.

"You'd get a buzz out of Dinosaur Park and the Trolley Barn Mall," he said, in a convincing tone. "Of course, there are skyline drives, canyons, and the great salt flats. Downtown Salt City is cool with the Mormon Temple and the Tabernacle to make you gasp. If you have time, I'll wheel you around the capital city."

Mrs. Zavitz heard his offer. Clearing her throat, she raised her eyebrows and conspicuously stared at Jerry.

Sandy saved the moment again. Pressing her tongue into her cheek, she nodded toward Mrs. Z, and said, "You'll have to ask our coach. I'll introduce you."

Leaning forward, she hoped to change Mrs. Z's agitated expression.

"Mrs. Zavitz. This is Jerry Chadwick from Utah and Michigan State. Jerry, this is our coach."

Mrs. Z gracefully admitted that she had been listening to parts of our conversation.

"I've caught bits of your sales talk," she said. "So Utah is your home, but you attend MSU. Tell me about that?"

Jerry's answer was forthright.

"I'm on a swimming scholarship. Political science is my major. I'm a Mormon, so after I graduate, I plan to spend my first two years in church work." He hesitated and then asked, "Have you been to Utah before?"

"Oh, yes. I remember it well," answered Mrs. Z. "I was driving my dad's new car and pulling a camper. In Provo, I misread a road sign. Making a wrong turn in mountainous terrain was not too smart. The road became gravel, then wound like a snake for ten miles or so up a canyon wall. There were no turnabouts. Finally, I arrived at the Mountain Meadow Ranch and turned into the barnyard. Two Doberman pinchers met me at the front door, ugly as sin and wanting to tear me to shreds."

"Panic attack," I screeched. "What then?"

"You can be sure I didn't stay to play Frisbee with those white-fanged canines. I high-tailed it back to the car. Without permission from the rancher, I made a U-turn in a cloud of dust. I drove down that buggy trail, bumping and bouncing like a prairie wagon. As you kids would say, I smoked."

"That must have been before cement became king of the road," said Jerry. "Our highways are now paved and extra wide. There are turnabouts at every lookout. I was born and grew up in Tooele, a city southwest of the capital. I know the territory by heart. I could almost drive blindfolded in the Wasatch Mountains and find my way home."

"Those qualifications are impressive," offered Mrs. Z. "Tell you what. On Sunday, before our flight home, the morning is free. Go ahead and plan a local tour. Pick up the girls at the Motor Hotel in Temple Square and deposit them at the airport by one o'clock."

Sandy whispered, "Wow! Bonus points, partner. We get to sight-see."

"Bring your seats to an upright position and note the seat belt sign," said the stewardess. "We're beginning our descent."

The plane pitched tail high, and for a second, I felt weightless, totally freed from gravity's pull.

"Feels like our pilot is a stunt flyer," joked Jerry. "Sure hope he makes a soft landing."

Tearing a small piece of paper from the nausea bag in the seat pocket, Jerry scribbled some numbers and handed the note to Sandy.

"Here's my phone number to use in case there's a snag in our Sunday plan. As for Saturday, I'll be at the pool, but I doubt if we get to talk. I'm betting you two and the ABC sports announcer will be tied up in an interview. Winners are always on camera."

He and Sandy exchanged smiles warm enough to melt a glacier.

As the plane came to a halt, everyone around us

smushed together in the aisle. Jerry was lucky. He moved toward the exit with little delay.

"Look for our greeter," said Mrs. Zavitz. "Someone from the transportation committee will meet us."

Once inside the ramp, Sandy hurried me like a marathon walker. I think she wanted to keep Jerry in here sight. Bursting through the tunnel, we both saw a sign, USSS, bouncing like a yo-yo and heard a voice calling.

"Aquarians. I'm over here," shouted our hostess. A really big roly-poly lady came rushing toward us.

"I'm Jolene Spitz," she said in a voice that sounded like she had a rag rug in her throat. "Don't look surprised. I'm not related to the world-famous Mark. He was my heart-throb when I was your age. His black hair and broad shoulders . . . I tell you, girls, he was a handsome buck."

I turned sober faced trying to understand "buck." I think she meant macho or sexy.

"You know who I mean, don't you?" she asked, sounding persistent.

Sandy answered. "He was Mr. Gold Medal at the Olympics years ago."

Patting my partner on her shoulder, our effervescent greeter said, "You have that right, Sandy. I know your name from the picture my daughter has in her room. My darling Marla wants to be just like you, a solo champion. Some day your coach may train my polliwog."

Sandy and I glanced at each other with quiet snickers in our noses. Mrs. Spitz's friendliness tickled our fancy bones. I was next to receive this lady's Western hospitality. I felt the message when she wrapped me in a tight bear hug. I could have sprinted a pool lap while being cuddled like a stuffed toy.

"Here is Julie Jacobs," she said, as if speaking to a celebrity. "You are the biggest threat of the year, so I've been told by the local swimmers. News of your entry in this meet hit our papers, big time. You must be sensational. Our budding athletes have named you The Gold Nugget."

"You can't be serious," I screeched. "Nobody knows me at this level of competition."

"Oh! But they know your partner and your coach," said Mrs. Spitz. "That combo is superior. We figure you are Sandy's ace partner . . . a real winner."

Mrs. Z appeared looking colossal in her uniform. She carried a cassette case that held our music and a business folder filled with synchro documents. She was a VIP in the sport: chairman of the rules committee, head of judges training and a national judge, herself.

"Welcome, Helen, to Mormon territory," said Mrs. Spitz. "It's good to see you and these two gems you brought along. Please, give me your luggage tags. I have a fellow who will claim and deliver your cases to the hotel. My car is waiting, so follow along."

Two by two, we made our way to the parking lot and settled into a compact car about one-third the size of our van. All the way across town, Mrs. Spitz talked about Utah. In her gravel voice, strangling every word, we learned the facts.

"This is grid city. Our streets are one hundred thirty-two feet wide."

For a moment, she took her hands off the wheel to accentuate width. I tightened my seat belt.

"Utah was the forty-fifth state to join the Union," she said, proudly. "It's the Beehive state."

She was now speeding like I think they do on the salt flats, or, when one of those bees lodge in a driver's underpants.

"We have the oldest dinosaur quarry in the world. Our caves have helictites growing straight outward from the walls. You will love this Rocky Mountain territory. It's a land of splendor."

I whispered to Sandy. "It's a land of at least one supersonic driver."

X

Headquarters Hotel

The sun was in the western sky as we arrived at the head-quarters hotel. In a merry manner, Mrs. Z waved good-bye to Mrs. Spitz, our bullet speedster. Turning to face Sandy and me, Coach Zavitch displayed her good nature in a bouquet of words. "This meet could be the start of something grand."

Closing one eye, she focused down a sight to an unknown target, a secret yet to be revealed.

"You girls will make it happen. I can feel it in the air. In all my coaching years, I have never entered a duet in nationals with the potential you two bring to this meet."

With that compliment, my chest inflated. I was airborne soaring over the city like a balloon. My legs wanted to spring and my arms wanted to fling, but to appear more mature, I looked up at the six flags snapping above my head in the mountain air. I gave a quick salute.

We three, standing ready for the contest of the year, wore smiles worth more than a million gold nuggets.

Inside the hotel a banner hung above the lobby. Large letters identified the big event; "U.S. Senior Championship for Duet Synchronized Swimmers." I repeated the title over and over in my mind, feeling triumphant even before I had competed.

The lobby resembled a walk-in undersea grotto. The

Hospitality Committee had decorated with massive shapes of coral, sea anemones, fronds and ferns. My first glimpse of the fish in the glass tank made me both happy and homesick. Jake's and Jude's relatives were there but not in yellow and blue costumes.

The registration clerk handed out freebie packets, room card-keys, and identification tags. Pointing to the mail room, she said, "Your practice schedule and the program of events are in a mail box marked Aquarius."

Mrs. Z collected her packet and key for room two-twenty. Sandy and I had keys for room 222.

"Go ahead and unpack," said Mrs. Z. "I'll pick up the mail. Eat dinner here in the hotel with other swimmers. Remember we are on Mountain Time. Curfew is ten o'clock. I'll be in meetings 'til nine or so. Don't miss the fun planned for the swimmers in the Wasatch room. A telepathist is on stage . . . an unbelievable mind reader. Expect to be spooked by an Anasazi Indian. See you at breakfast."

Sandy and I hurried up the stairs to the second floor. Our room was halfway down the hall. Opening the door, Sandy stepped in cheering, "The Toads pad for three super days."

We rollicked around in the room, checked the bathroom, the view out the window, and claimed a twin bed.

"Forget unpacking," chirped Sandy. "Let's dress in our club sweats and go see the water witch. She sounds cool."

The Wasatch room was buzzing with voices. As Sandy and I entered the room, about forty swimmers were sitting in a powwow circle waiting for the psyche to arrive. Two look alike girls were the first to greet us.

"Over here, Michigan. Sit with us," hollered one. I had seen these swimmers before. Then it hit me. They were the White Doves. Those two identical syncs with wading-bird legs had been my idol. Their music, costumes, and choreography had flamed my desire to swim tandem. There they sat, fair skinned, blondes with blue eyes that squinched into laughing slits. They were the real queens of duets. Feeling like my chances as a goddess had been diluted, I slowly followed Sandy across the floor.

"Julie, meet Sheli and Keli Conners, my rivals in solo and now in duets," said Sandy. "These two will show the judges incredible choreography."

"Incredible luck," said Sheli. "That's what we'll need in this pool. Racing blocks fill up the deck on one side, and there is a movable bulkhead on the other."

"Some pools are like that," said Sandy. "I gave a demonstration at Michigan State University, in a pool built for speed and diving. We can handle it."

"But, Sandy," continued Sheli, "the bottom is crisscrossed with black lines."

"If that's what we have here," answered Sandy, "Mrs. Z will solve the problem. You can be sure, her one and only entry in this meet is not going to get lost under the bulkhead." Sandy sounded so convincing I should have been at ease, but my breath stopped, my brain rebelled, and I stomped my foot like an impetuous child.

"What else can happen to me?" I growled. "I've waited for a female body, spent months hunting for vertical, licked the dizzies, been willing to grunt in place of breathing, and now, to avoid an impending disaster, I need a navigator's license. I'd die, absolutely die, if I came to the surface after a spin and swam off like a lost soloist."

"We'll fix it," decreed Sandy, sounding like a judge in court. "Markers can be used as spot check points. This dilemma is solvable."

A tom-tom thundered as we took our places in the circle. A beautiful Anasazi American Indian woman entered the room. In a doeskin dress with strands of flowing beads, she moved with liquid grace about us with soft moccasin steps. Her silky black hair cascaded over her shoulders like a shawl. With an easiness of manner, she introduced herself.

"My name is Vana. I am a descendant of the Anasazi Indians. My people lived in this Bonneville Valley long ago before the white man came." Her eyes twinkled with merriment as she continued. "I'm beginning this pow wow with show and tell."

She spread a multicolored rug in the center of our circle. On it she placed a basket bursting with colors of red, yellow, orange, and green. A vase of pottery was last to be displayed.

"I do not intend to present an evening of Indian arts and crafts," she said. "I just want you to see what my great-great-grandma had accomplished by the time she was your age; a teenager with unique talent."

Looking at us with a softness of understanding, she said, "I doubt if any one of you could make any one of these items here on the floor. To be honest, girls, I can't either. We wouldn't take the time to weave a rug or make a basket. Nowadays we rush to a store and buy ready-mades."

Laughter rippled in her throat as she continued, "The good old days are worlds away from the here and now. For example. A teenage Indian maiden sent a message to her brave by smoke signals after rubbing two sticks and setting a fire. You gals can fax love notes in minutes to your special guy even if he lives in Nome, Alaska."

"She's a riot," I said to Sandy while everyone was laughing.

"I've been told," said the Indian, "you synchro swimmers are like fish, born to swim. Your duffles are overflowing with beautiful aquatic skills. People call you the crafty athletes."

That remark described what we all lived up to.

Vana continued. "I have a strange mysterious craft, a brain that receives thought waves of other people."

Her brown eyes grew anxious for our reaction to that impossible remark. Not one swimmer made a noise even though her announcement stirred up a kind of mental hysteria.

"I've been labeled the Wireless Witch, the Wasatch Wave, and Voodoo Vana," said the American Indian, "but I hope you girls will think of me as the Artiste Anasazi. Let's test my talent. Someone volunteer to start us off."

Hands flew upward, including mine. Vana pointed to me.

"All right, Ms. Aquarius. Think of another talent other than synchro that you have in your bag of tricks, something you are trained to do. In one word, whisper it to the girl sitting on your right and on your left."

Cupping my hands, I whispered "dancing" into Sandy's ear and then to the swimmer wearing a monogrammed jacket, Cygnet of San Antonio.

With closed eyes, Vana slowly tilted and twisted her neck like a TV antenna.

"Keep saying the word to yourself," said Vana. "Help me receive your thought."

The room grew silent. All eyes shuttled and rolled in doubtful faces. Slowly the seconds ticked on the clock. I repeated the word "dancing" to my brain at least fifty times. As if in a trance, Vana began to sway and glide. She performed a ballet sequence I had danced a hundred times in front of the mirror.

"Dancing is your craft," she said with confidence. "It has served you well when creating exceptional choreography."

I had trouble controlling my voice as I answered, "Yes,

that is true." My mind had been dumped into twisting turbulence and I wanted to scream for help.

"There is time for one more brain teaser," said Vana. "Who's next?"

A petite girl from Santa Clara, California, jumped to her feet.

"Guess my craft," she coaxed.

"My pleasure," said Vana. "After I leave the room, tell all these doubting swimmers your craft so everyone can participate." Vana quickly disappeared into the hall.

In a whisper of exaggerated lip movements, the word "gymnastics" was breathed around the room 'til everybody understood.

"We're ready," hollered the Californian.

Without delay, Vana came billowing back into the room like a ghost-ridden cloud.

"Think the word, girls," urged the Indian. "Send me a strong signal."

Again the room hushed. Only those invisible brain waves filled the air. Minutes passed as Vana settled into deep concentration. Then, as if her Indian sun god had beamed the signal, she began to speak in a rhyming rhythm.

You can tumble on the mat,
You can swing around the bar.
You can balance on the beam
Like the gymnast that you are.

Frowns appeared on our faces as we sat dumbfounded in the pow wow circle. I gazed into space with one eye open as my mouth shaped a huge hole.

"No way," I said to Sandy. "She isn't for real. We've been spooked. She can't hook up with somebody's thoughts. Unbelievable."

Vana didn't offer to explain or answer questions. She let us sit there, steeping in her bag of tricks while trying to stir up something that made sense.

"Now you have a brief sample of my crafty talent. I'll come to the pool to see yours," she said.

My brain needed a quick escape from the voodoo room and my insides craved for food. An embarrassing growl from my stomach announced my condition.

"Who's starving?" asked Keli.

"Julie Jacobs," I answered in a state of mental muddle.

"Let's hit the coffee shop," said Keli, urging us to move out.

We four went bounding down the hall like ballet dancers. The scent of fresh coffee directed out path. With empty stomachs we arrived at the shop and settled into the first empty table. A waitress soon appeared carrying a small black kettle in her hand.

"Will you be ordering our special or from the chef's kettle of mixes? With either order, you are served black crickets."

With that sickening announcement, I gagged on a swallow of air. Did she mean real crickets that once were alive? I didn't dare to ask. Sandy and the Conner girls sat speechless with faces masked in tragedy, so they didn't help. For sure, I was suspicious about the mix in that black kettle hanging near my nose. Probably bees and bugs were floating around in a salt brine. Selecting the least of the evils, I gingerly inquired, "What's in the special?"

"It's Anasazi bean soup and buffalo burgers," answered the waitress. "A mile-high dessert of multiflavored ice cream comes with the special."

As if we swimmers were performing as a team, together we chimed, "FOUR SPECIALS, PLEASE!"

The waitress eased our cricket shock by casually saying, "You will want to read the cricket story on the back of the dessert menu."

Sandy snatched the menu and read aloud.

In 1848 crickets made a massive invasion into Utah. They ate the stems and stalks of the crops planted by the Mormons. Restaurants were forced to go out of business because of the food shortage. As the people prayed for help, clouds of sea gulls flew in and devoured the crickets. God was given credit for the miracle. The gulls represented God's ability to overcome adversity with good. A monument to honor the gulls stands in downtown Salt Lake City. Restaurant owners keep the miracle in the minds of Utah citizens by serving candy crickets.

When the specials were served, the crickets arrived, too.

"Compliments of the Salt Water Candy Company," said the waitress, placing a dish of black bugs on the table.

"These black candies are really sweet and sticky confections. You'll remember their meaning forever. Hop to it, girls."

We stared at the bugs while spooning our soup, then, for the first time in our lives, ate ground buffalo. Just when I felt comfortable with the taste of my sandwich, which was a cool burger almost as good as a Big Mac, Sandy teasingly said, "Be sure you chew up the dinosaur tails in the Anasazi soup."

With the witchcraft baffling our minds and black crickets hopping around inside our stomachs, we headed for our rooms, hoping to snooze through the night.

XI

The Deseret Pool

As I opened one eye, I saw slots of morning daylight making lines on the bedroom wall. Sandy was out of bed and in the bathroom. I heard a gentle knocking at our door and a voice calling, "Wake up, girls. Breakfast in a half hour."

Opening the door, our petite coach stepped in, wearing an all-white uniform. She was dressed to judge the afternoon competition.

"Breakfast in the coffee shop and then off to the pool for figure practice," she said.

Hearing the word "figure" caused a momentary conflict between my confidence and fear, but I put on a happy face and greeted Coach Zavitz with a cheerful, "Good morning."

Sandy emerged from the bathroom, upbeat and anxious.

"We're going to cruise through figures," she said, parading her confidence in a peacock strut as she crossed the room.

"Catch these newspaper headlines," said Mrs. Z, opening the sports section across my bed.

"Aquarius Poised for Gold. Now that says it all and then some."

One look at the photo charged me with happiness. My sophisticated expression was more like a twenty-year-old

New York model. Back home, Mrs. Z's makeup artist had worked magic on my features before sending our publicity prints to Utah. Even my own mother could have been fooled.

After dressing in club sweats and stuffing our totes, we were on our way. My mouth worked overtime telling Mrs. Z about incredible Vana. Coach Zavitz absorbed every word and exhaled a sigh of disbelief.

"Vana's craft is mystifying and unbelievable," she said. "I suggest you douse that eerie episode into the trough before it floods your mind with fake thoughts. Vana makes money by baffling her audience. She's a Las Vegas entertainer."

Dying to tell the cricket story, jokingly, Sandy told Mrs. Z that we ate black bugs for dinner.

"I've prescribed many diets for swimmers but never black bugs," responded Mrs. Z. "It sounds like we three had an unusual and challenging evening. My meeting presented a terrific opportunity." Pressing her hands together as if to pray, she paused dramatically before going on with her story.

"How would you girls like to spend six weeks in Europe with me next summer?"

"WOW! That sounds fantabulous," I exploded. "To sightsee or swim?" Mrs. Z's eyes grew excited and my heart pounded as she laid out the plan.

"I've been asked to assemble eighteen elite swimmers to go abroad to promote our sport. Demonstrations and training clinics will be scheduled in six or seven foreign countries. European swim clubs like ours will house and feed us once we get there."

"Toads on tour," shouted Sandy. "Kings, queens, and the Crystal Palace pool in London. Before my career ends, I want to swim in that natatorium for the Royal Family."

"You may get your wish," said Mrs. Z, "but don't broadcast this trip, yet. There are many wrinkles to iron out. Keep the secret until the official announcement is made."

I hugged Sandy and she squeezed me. Screaming little squeaks like we do underwater, we celebrated our secret one year in advance.

"Let's get to the pool," I cheered. "I'm ready to swim the Atlantic."

Hurriedly, we left the coffee shop and headed for the shuttle van that transported swimmers and officials to the pool.

During a ten-minute ride, we saw the city sights. The Mormon Temple, with its gray granite spires, stood in all its holiness facing the widest street I had ever seen. Moments later, the state capitol dominated the landscape. In the distance, the Wasatch Mountains were trimmed with a ribbon of light from the rising sun.

"Everything is huge out here," I exclaimed, as our vehicle moved into a wide circular drive.

The pool building stretched nearly a city block. Flagpoles in a row, stood like color guards. Long curving steps of granite gave us a wide welcome. Step by step, I climbed to the door of the Deseret pool. To my left stood a statue of King Neptune guarding the natatorium's entrance. To my right and above my head, hung a humanlike sculpture with its back arched and its arms outstretched in a swan dive. There, in the presence of myth and human achievement, I was ready to dance on the water.

Once inside, we rushed to an opening from which music was flowing. Catching a glimpse of the room, I shouted, "Humungus! This isn't a pool, it's part of Great Salt Lake. I'll get lost."

Seeing those criss-crossed black lines, Sandy shouted, "It's an aquatic stage for tic-tac-toe. Don't worry, partner.

We'll X-out the other players. Come on, champ. Let's find the locker room."

A blue door at the shallow end of the pool kept opening and closing as swimmers came and went.

"This way," said Sandy, moving toward the busy exit. I tailed along, not wanting to miss anything in the huge room. Looking up I saw the broadcast booth with two television cameras poised for action. Another camera was mounted on the three meter board. The bulkhead seemed to be in place dividing the pool in half. Five ladder highchairs were spaced around the competitive area. Flashes of light came from an underwater window. I guess people were down there taking pictures of swimmers instead of sharks and rays.

We entered the locker room to find a posh lounge with private dressing rooms. Swimmers could claim a roomette for dressing and relax in a lounge equipped with mirrors, comfortable sofas, game tables, and a big screen television set.

Sandy found a vacant room, and we popped in to claim our own little pad.

"Let's wear our jungle print," she said, pulling one of three tank suits from her duffle. Her suggestion hit my happy spot. I was ready to wear something wild to match the free spirit flitting about inside my body. Clawing through my duffle, I found the right suit. After stripping to nakedness as if my clothes were on fire, I had only to wiggle and pull before becoming a tiger ready to pounce.

"Hit the liquid, champ," I shouted.

Plunging through the curtain and then the door to the pool, I was off on a maiden voyage. With a pair of nose clips tucked under my pant leg, I let myself down into the water. Slowly I soaked all over as goose bumps attacked my skin. Pushing off from the wall, I cut through the wet stuff like a sailboat in a high wind. The color blue sparkled all around me, and I felt weightless.

"Water, water, water," I said to the friendly waves. "My home away from home."

In the huge pool, female swimmers were like schools of fish darting up and down eight lanes of crystal clear water. Tanned by the California sun, their slim minnow shapes met me both going and coming.

Sandy caught up with me at the end of our lane.

"We sure are washed out and lily white," she said. "I feel anemic. These West Coast girls are so bronze tan. We're snow queens compared to them." Smile-wrinkles formed at the corners of her eyes and she cupped her hands, packed a make-believe snowball, and tossed it at me.

We finished our warm-ups and joined Mrs. Z on the other side of the bulkhead. It was figure critique time, and I was ready no matter how many repeats my coach would demand.

A crowd of young swimmers sat watching us practice, their eyes avidly drinking in our technique and their ears recording Mrs. Z's coaching tips. They clapped when Sandy finished and took pictures of my double ballet legs. As we climbed out of the pool, those young budding athletes pleaded for our autographs.

"I haven't won anything yet," I announced to the group. Regardless of my lack of fame, their optimism had to be satisfied, so I scribbled "Julie Jacobs" until every fan, wild with happiness, turned away.

Billowing bubbles boiled the water near where we had been practicing. An underwater photographer came to the surface and asked if we would stay on and do some stunts for the camera. Mrs. Z asked a few questions before granting permission.

"Whom do you represent and how do you plan to use the footage?"

"I'm a member of ABC's crew here to televise this competition," he answered. "Please, Madam. I need more footage to use as background when America is introduced to this event. I have film of the defending champions, but the jungle-print suits your girls are wearing will add to the show."

That remark brought a deadpan look of disinterest on Sandy's face, but she was a good sport. Obviously, he did not know Sandy was the U.S. solo champion.

In a flat voice, lacking patience, Mrs. Z said, "Quickly, girls. Do a chain dolphin and then we must go." Slipping into the water, Sandy connected her feet to my head. The photographer submerged under my feet. Sandy led the chain, forming a circlelike design. The stunt was so simple that I had time to mouth "Hi, Mom" and "Hi, Dad" as I faced the camera. We repeated the circle, so I said, "Hi, Jake" and "Hi, Jude" the second time around.

Before the photographer made it to the surface, Sandy and I were out of the pool. He came up laughing as he removed his goggles.

"Tell me, do blowfish faces and crossed eyes go with that stunt?" he asked. Shrugging my shoulders, I gazed at Sandy for the answer. She didn't say a word, but her wide-eyed expression didn't fool me. I had discarded puffy cheeks way back in my early training and I crossed my eyes only when my nose clips leaked. Snickering inside ourselves, we thanked the cameraman for admiring our jungle print suits.

Dripping wet, we headed for the shower room. In a low voice, Sandy said, "In no way will those dolphin circles make national television. When the editor sees my face, he'll die of horror." I kept mum about saying hi to my parents and to my pets.

Once inside the shower room, we discovered it to be a ritzy spa. There were tanks of water labeled mountain minerals. The room was equipped with water jets in the walls, in the floor, and above my head. Sandy sat in a hot tank until she turned red, then high-stepped to a cold one and stayed until the shivers set in.

"What a blast," she shouted.

I romped about being sprayed on all my body parts. My toes and fingers tingled as the forceful water spewed at me. Wet bullets of cold water hit my back as I slowly turned around. I released a scream that would have awakened the dead.

We dipped and doused as minutes passed until a voice came over the intercom: "Figure competition will begin at two o'clock. All competitors immediately report to the Deseret lounge. The drawing for the order of performance will begin in ten minutes."

"That's for us," said Sandy. "Let's scramble. We may be the first to draw 'cause it's done alphabetically by club name."

After dressing in our Aquarius sweats, we joined the rush of swimmers heading for the lounge.

There were partners dressed in pink sweats from the Florida Flamingo Club and two tall girls in green from the Shamrock Corketts of Texas. The only black Americans in the room were from New York. They were dressed in shades of peachy coral. Had this been a beauty contest, they would have won the crown. Their dark eyes, black hair, and light-brown-sugar complexions caused us all to admire their Jamaican features. Of course, Sandy and I added a refreshing splash of turquoise to the mix. The Newark Naiads had chosen to wear white sweats with red lettering and the

Dayton Dolphin swimmers, dressed in shimmering blue-purple, caused my lips to quietly say "expensive."

We greeted each other with crossed fingers and a back-and-forth hand wave, a sign everybody in synchro knew meant good luck in the draw. Every swimmer wanted to draw the lucky numbers from thirteen to forty. That's because the scores from the judges usually increased after a dozen performances.

A lady dressed in red, white, and blue sat at a table near the back of the lounge. She was the national president of synchro. A name plate identified her title. On the table, a fish bowl filled with small pirouette rolls of paper contained the numbers we were to draw. Mrs. Z sat next to the president poised to conduct the event. Pleased to see Sandy and me, she gave us a heart-lifting smile that helped to ease my dithers.

"The Aquarius club girls will draw first," said Mrs. Z. "Julie Jacobs and then Sandy Jenkins, please select numbers from the fish bowl."

With my every step toward the table, I could feel the room tingling with wishes. All the swimmers were secretly praying for number one to be drawn.

Mrs. Z winked at me as if to say, "Brave up to it. You have the best chance of all." I dunked my hand into the bowl and pinched a pencilike roll of paper. Unrolling it, I saw my lucky number.

"Twenty-five," I cheered and made a few Macarena body moves to punctuate my delight. Low groans filled the room from those whose nerves were grating.

Sandy announced her number with a joyous voice. "Number forty and last but not least," she said, hardily in a sportive tone.

Mrs. Z recorded our luck in the draw and then made an announcement. "Listen up, everyone. After you have drawn a number, go to the trophy room for a buffet lunch. Return to the pool at two o'clock for figure competition."

Happy with our order of performance, we were in the mood to celebrate. I wanted to hit the spa again, but Sandy's stomach was growling for food. She was always hungry.

"Let's find the chow," she said in a plaintive voice as we left the lounge and wound our way along the halls.

In the spacious trophy room, awards of past and present Deseret swimmers were on display. A team photo, dated nineteen twenty-five, showed girls wearing knicker-type suits.

"They sure look funny in pants that balloon from the waist to the knees," I said to Sandy. "How did they stay afloat in all that wet fabric?"

Another photo of boys wearing bodysuits reminded us of the first layer of clothing Michigan skiers snuggle into before going up the slopes.

"No wonder swimming records improved as swimsuit styles changed," said Sandy. "Hurrah for weightless Lycra spandex! We're lucky to be competitors in the new millennium."

We syncs were anxious to taste the spread of tantalizing finger foods, so we began by stuffing our cheeks like chipmunks do when nuts are around. I sampled a wedge of pizza that moistened into a mouthful of glue. A cup of soup helped to wash it down. Just as I found the pecan tarts, Sheli Conners broadcast news I was happy to hear.

"The checkerboard pool now has colored sides. Strips of plastic hang from the trough like wallpaper. A red stripe is on one side, a green on another, and across from the bulkhead, the stripe is yellow."

I flashed a smile, happy to know we could guide by color.

"Sounds like a traffic light," I said to Sandy. "Come on.

Let's go see and stake out our deck space. One More Time needs a pad with a good view."

Pointing at the tarts in my hand, Sandy said, jokingly, "No food allowed on deck, Jacobs. You can't bribe the judges with tarts."

Pushing the thumb-size desserts into my mouth like a handful of popcorn, I left the trophy room.

Back in the amazing dressing room, I slithered into a black tank suit, the required garb for figure competition. The little bump in my pant leg was really an extra pair of nose clips. My performance clip, the one that fit and wouldn't leak, was on my finger. Most girls had long hair like I did, so ponytails and braids were popular.

The pool room was beginning to look like a beach party. Towels were spread in a patchwork design on the deck. Sandy and I unloaded our duffles, spilling puzzles, pictures and, of course, our toads onto the pad.

"Before my nerves begin to shake and rattle, I'm opening Todd's gift," I announced. I quickly untied the shoelace bow and opened the tiny jewel box to see Buddha's present.

"It's a good-luck charm. A silver shamrock," I shouted. "There's a silver chain, too. Help me put it on, partner. I want to wear it in figure competition."

"Look into the box again, Julie. There's probably a note," said Sandy.

Sure enough, a piece of paper folded into a tiny cube came along with the gift.

"Get this, Sandy," I said, reading out loud: "A lucky necklace for a goddess."

I wanted to dance and shout but didn't dare to make a scene, so I muffled a squeal and sat bubbling in happiness.

People were streaming into the balcony and the judges were gathering on deck. Mrs. Z acting as clerk of the course, readied the scoring table and seated the judges.

Sandy and I started our stretching exercises. We could bend like a pretzel and split our legs flat to the floor, front to back and side to side.

"Look effortless, Jacobs," I said to myself. "When you hit the water, glide like a duck."

Mrs. Z's whistle of three short blasts announced the magic moment. Contestant number one, wearing a fake smile for those stone-faced judges, took a motionless layout on the water surface. We syncs gave her a hand clap of confidence as the pool began to talk its special language. A thin sheet of water flowed into the trough making babylike gurgles. Rings of wavelets rippled across the pool.

In less than a half hour, I would be performing the Flamingo spinning three sixty.

"One chance, J.J." I said to myself, "to perform that dizzy-doozy stunt. One chance to perform like Sandy, a real champion." Clutching Todd's good luck charm, I prayed, "Oh, God. Help me through figures."

High scores, sevens and upward were awarded the swimmers ahead of me. I needed eights to keep up with Sandy. Her score and mine would be added together. Our average became part of our total score when added to the routine.

All the elements of figure competition burning in my brain began to cry out: be smooth, be effortless, keep a steady rhythm, hold a high water line, extend the legs, point the toes, hit plumb, show flexibility, breath silently, and sell confidence to the judges.

"You better be perfect," I ordered myself.

A glance at One More Time helped me to handle the moment. My mascot was wearing a smile of endless inspiration. He was speaking to me like my dad, who never let me sink into defeat.

"Do your best, one more time."

The referee called my number. Sandy gave me a hug and a high five.

"Go for it, partner. Blow 'em away," she whispered.

After swallowing her advice, my mouth turned dry. Slipping my clips into place, I poised with confidence as my mom had taught.

"Dance through this, girl. Your debut is for real," I said quietly.

"Swimmer number twenty-five," repeated the referee. "The figure is Double Ballet Legs."

I floated on my back with ease. No teeter-totter trouble.

"Go," said the ref.

Under my hands, little funnels of beadlike bubbles worked downward, supplying uplift to support a ton, so it seemed. With both legs in the air and nine feet of liquid below me, gravity screamed, "Sink, sink, sink." But that invisible force couldn't beat me. Mrs. Z's rookie swimmer was in control. Finishing according to the handbook description changed those stone faces to a smile.

"Scores, please," requested the referee.

I waited without breathing.

"Eights across the board," she said.

Sandy screeched into a wadded towel, and more fans than I ever imagined clapped approval. My spirits soared to the top of the Wasatch Mountains.

"Supercalafabulistic," I heard my mom say as my widening eyes responded to that splendiferous surprise.

"The next figure is a Flamingo spinning three sixty," said the referee.

After the signal to go, I easily moved through the required positions. I hit plumb and spun three hundred and sixty degrees, with my toes holding at the center of the spin. Feeling as happy as Jake and Jude in their aquarium, I slowly headed for the bottom. The dizzy doozy figure felt my very best ever. As I surfaced, the referee read the scores.

"Eight point five, eight point three, and the remaining scores are eight point five."

I had to scream or burst, so I dipped under and hollered, "YAH-HOO."

Sandy had it right when she said we would cruise through figures. Her performance was flawless, and the camera would show it to the world. I finished in fifth place and she in first. At the end of figure competition, we were two-tenths of a point behind Sheli and Keli Conners, the defending champions. I had a feeling all four of us would make headlines in the news. My folks would go ape.

Darting like hummingbirds, we whisked up our belongings and disappeared in an air of excitement.

The ride back to the hotel was a blast. The jam-packed van was loaded with cackling girls, relieved to know the dreaded event was over. The Conner twins were wearing grins a yard wide and bouncing with the thought of defending their title.

"One down and one to go," I said with more confidence than ever before. "Tomorrow is gold rush day."

Above our chatter, Mrs. Z's voice rang out as she high-stepped into the van.

"Where's that Midwestern power pack?" she asked, as her eyes sparkled like stars. "Congratulations, girls. You are *awesome!* An olympian production."

XII

Super Saturday

Our Saturday in the Rockies began at sunrise.

"Dress in your travel uniform," said Sandy. "Breakfast first, then the parade."

Whipping my towel at her, I said just for fun, "Let's order grasshoppers for breakfast. I'll need another miracle to survive this day."

After packing my new tote with enough stuff to supply a K-Mart store, I was ready to hit the road. Mrs. Z was waiting for us in the hall, primed with the day's schedule.

"Good morning, Toads," she quipped. "We're eating with Coach Re Calcaterra and the Conner twins. After breakfast the fun begins. You four swimmers will lead the parade, riding in white convertibles."

"VIP day again," I cheered.

Sandy answered with a tinge of superiority, "More like crowning day for queens."

The coffee shop was a hive of buzzing swimmers. Brown bodies from California sat laughing in shouts attracting attention. The New York girls were flirting with the waiters, and the Florida bunch stood in juice lines, posing like pink flamingos.

"Join us," shouted Mrs. Calcaterra, waving her arms.

"Good morning, champs," said Mrs. Z as she walked up to the twins. "This is the day of days. Make your mark again at this meet and a colossal experience is yours. I'm sure you and your coach know what I'm talking about. Right, Cal?"

Beaming with joy, Coach Cal answered, "Next summer's tour in Europe was too good to keep secret from my girls. I let the good news out before the twins competed in figures."

"We'd die to go!" exclaimed Keli.

"Wow! Would we," shouted Sheli.

Surges of excitement shot through my body as I realized the twins were going, too.

"All right," I shrieked. "I'd love to be on tour with you guys."

"Here's the scoop," said Coach Cal. "The tour group will be called The American Aquacade. Divers, maybe a gymnast, dancers and of course, solo, duet and team syncs will make up our company. The synchro girls will double as dancers. I have a country folk routine in my repertoire called the Tennessee Wig Walk. With your background, Julie, you'll love it. It's a show stopper, choreographed for ten dancers in a chorus line."

Hearing that, I bubbled and spouted my happiness until, with great earnestness, Coach Zavitz turned my excitement toward the events of the day.

"Focus on the here and now," she said. "You girls need to swim in this pool at the top of your talent before sticking your toes into foreign water."

Sandy answered with a convincing tone, "Count on us, Coach. We'll do our best, one more time."

We caught the shuttle van to the pool and joined other athletes for the city parade. At least ten convertibles were lined up in the circular drive awaiting America's top duets. As we dashed for car number one, the fresh mountain air gave spring to our steps and colored our cheeks red. We felt like climbing the Wasatch Mountains, but instead, we climbed aboard our white chariot and perched two by two facing center.

"Wish I had something to toss our fans along the way," said Sheli.

"You do," answered Keli. "Throw 'em a kiss from that million-dollar smile you learned from me."

Hearing that remark, our young movie star driver turned and gazed admiringly at Sheli, probably hoping he would catch her first kiss.

The serpentine line of cars left the pool with all of us cheering, "USA—USA."

School kids along the way were wearing that glad last day of school expression as they waved a spirited welcome. I felt the tingly atmosphere all around me.

As we entered the main part of town, Sandy pointed her finger toward a window high up in a building. With a screech of surprise, she hollered, "LOOK! It's Jerry from flight 711. He's swinging Sparty from the end of a pole. See. There's MSU's mascot."

We all stood and hailed the lovable warrior.

The parade continued until our ears picked up the sound of voices singing "God Bless America." The music seemed to be coming from the Capitol grounds.

"You are hearing the Mormon Tabernacle Choir," said our driver. "It's the overture to the Governor's welcome."

Slowly, our convoy turned into the capitol drive, forming a necklace around the speaker's platform. As our motors silenced, a tall man stepped up to the microphone.

"I am Clifford Culver, mayor of Salt Lake City. It is my pride and pleasure to have a beautiful group of young ladies as our guests. For us, this occasion parallels the Miss America contest. The Utah residents congratulate you for your excellent achievements in Synchronized Swimming and wish you all the best of luck in tonight's final competition. Here to greet you is the governor of our great state, the Honorable Andrew Chadwick."

One look at this man charged Sandy's battery.

"Chadwick! Like Jerry?" she sparked. "Incredible? Am I seeing double? This man looks like Jerry and has the same last name. He's either Jerry's dad or his uncle."

"Quick. Ask our driver," I urged.

"You are right," answered the chauffeur. "Jerry is the governor's oldest son. He is studying political science at Michigan State University. The younger boy is at Tooele Academy."

Keli rocked in her seat with surprise.

"You know the governor's son?" she feverishly requested. "Are you dating him? Is he your boyfriend?"

"No, silly," answered Sandy. "We flew out here with him."

"Yah, and the big hunk sat next to me," I teased on purpose. "And get this. He is taking us to the Trolley Barn Mall and to the water slides."

Keli's and Sheli's eyes began popping, and they wanted more scoop about Jerry, but we had to stop talking and listen to the governor.

"This is the most outstanding gathering of beautiful athletes I have ever seen," said the governor. "You are America's queens of aquatics. I've been told you combine swimming, dancing, and gymnastics on a liquid stage.

"Tonight, my family and I will attend the finals to see your amazing skills. Thousands of people across this country will join us while watching 'ABC's Wide World of Sports.'

"Utah salutes America's synchro duets. As a memento of this championship, please accept a token from the organizing committee.

"God bless you and swim a peak performance."

Ladies in long gowns approached the cars carrying blue bags bursting with red-and-white tissue. The air was filled with sweet perfume as they smiled graciously and handed each of us a sack. I vibrated with excitement from the entire scene as the lady said, "Go for it. Down in the tissue."

Reaching into the bag, I found a real keeper.

"It's a glass paperweight," I cheered, holding a baseball-size crystal ball in my hand. "The Deseret natatorium is inside this bubble. What a neat keepsake."

"Very nice!" said Sandy. "A super collectible to remember a super city."

We all thanked our hostesses for our special gift.

"Sit tight, girls," said our driver as we slowly moved away from the state building. "We're heading back to the pool."

Sheli, in her friendly manner, continued to throw kisses until the cheering onlookers thinned away.

While gazing into my crystal ball, I saw an image. Not a queen, nor like Cinderella, a princess. I saw myself, a goddess, ready to prove my title to the world. My arms began to form those incredible patterns that Mom had created. Messages from my brain attacked my legs. Those gyrations from a year ago in the library wanted to jump out and run.

"Keep calm and be confident," I said to myself as if repeating Dad's exact words. But the event I loved most was just a few hours away and I could feel the pre-meet jitters shaking my hands.

At the natatorium, Coach Zavitz stood waiting for us. She had scheduled a rehearsal with the clerk of music.

"We're on in ten minutes," she said."I'll meet you deck-side at the music door."

Sandy and I zipped off to the locker room. In less than

ten minutes, we were dressed in turquoise tank suits with clips under our pant legs and on our fingers.

When we arrived at the music room, the clerk seemed out of breath and in need of CPR.

"Thank heavens you girls are on time," she said, forcing the words from a collapsed chest. From under her long limp hair, she introduced herself, "I'm Joyce Stromback, in charge of the music." Squinting at the list in her hand, she grumbled, "I'm determined to keep this mob of swimmers on schedule. Lord help me if I don't rehearse twenty routines before 3:00 P.M." Drawing a deep breath, she continued, "I was here until midnight last night. Some duets were a disaster. Swimmers lost their directions in this crossword puzzle pool. The coaches with liquid dynamite in their veins blew up like geysers. Notice, we have compass markings on the pool floor. North is shallow and south is deep. Do me a favor. Keep swimming to the music even if you head upstream instead of down."

With authority in her vice, Mrs. Z calmly instructed us to do what she wanted. "Take a minute, girls, to get your bearings. Lines or no lines, stick to your hourglass surface pattern and all will go well."

Sandy traced the pattern with her finger, saying, "Begin in the deep corner. Go diagonally shallow, then straight across the shallow end. Head deep on the second diagonal. Turn and swim facing the corner judge. Finish going diagonally shallow to about the middle of the pool. Don't puff, don't frown, and don't lose your clips."

Laughingly I repeated the pattern, feeling confident regardless of the black lines scoring the pool into squares.

With clips in place, we took our deck position. Sandy signaled to Mrs. Z and the music began. My willowy arms raised and lowered like a walking centipede and my head slithered back and forth across my shoulders. Bending our knees and ankles like frogs do in the water, we stepped toward the pool's edge. Together we dropped into space knifing downward through the liquid bubbles. There in the Deseret pool, my skills had a reunion. The flutter kick that Dad had taught to me gave this polliwog a powerful squirt. Mom's arm movements, the ones I had repeated in front of the mirror, were fluid and graceful. Mrs. Z's "one more time" business made the stunts easy to perform. Even the clumsy eggbeater kick supported me while I walked on the water.

Finishing the routine with spare energy and enough breath to do it again without a break, proved I had become a water mammal.

"Get ready for this critique," said Sandy, as Mrs. Zavitz motioned us over to the trough.

With Z's eyes rolling faster than our rewinding tape, she shouted, "Execute just like that tonight in the finals."

Joyce Stromback threw up her hands and cheered, "Hallelujah! Praise the Lord. After last night's rehearsal, I thought all coaches were disagreeable by nature. Wish you would stick around here and critique the next bunch."

XIII

The Finals

By the time we returned to the hotel for rest and relaxation, the sun had moved to the western sky and the mountains were costumed in pinkish purple.

Just minutes after flopping onto my bed, there came a knocking at our door. Sandy answered it.

"I have a forget-me-not bouquet for a goddess by the name of Sandy Jenkins," said the delivery guy. With wide eyes he asked, "Are you a goddess?"

Flashing a smile, Sandy answered, "That's me for tonight, the goddess of Siam." Shrugging her shoulders, she teased, "My fans are everywhere."

Bowing in respect for her deity, real or make-believe, the guy slowly backed away and headed down the hallway.

"Thanks for the flowers and cheers," she said before closing the door.

"Bet I know who sent these. Either Mrs. Spitz's daughter or—the governor's son," she shrieked.

"Quick, partner, read the card," I said excitedly, "before I turn green."

Opening the attached envelope, Sandy read the message. " 'See you at the crowning, Your Majesty.' It's signed 'Sparty, a humble servant.' " With a gleam in her eyes, she shouted, "This is Jerry's genius. He's so-o-o cool."

Admiringly, she placed the flowers in a drinking glass

on the night stand. I bounced on the bed, filled with the air of happiness.

Again, we tried to settle down and slow our rapid heartbeats, but the telephone added more excitement. I answered the ring to hear our parents say, "Hello, girls."

Holding the phone at my shoulder so Sandy could hear too, the message came loud and clear: "We wish you luck in the finals," they cheered in unison. Then Dad asked his usual question: "How's it going?"

With a shouting voice, I answered, "We're just two-tenths of a point behind the champions."

Dad's next remark was his way of saying things that always made me feel super.

"Give your routine the Jacobs and Jenkins know-how. The results will set a record."

"We've had a blast out here!" exclaimed Sandy. "The big news is Mrs. Z wants us to tour Europe next summer and give demonstrations."

Mom shouted, "Won't that be splendiferous?"

Next it was Mr. Jenkins's turn. In a voice full of chuckles, half serious with a fantastic idea, he inflated us with importance.

"We can't send Air Force One to bring you home, but we are willing to charter a plane for queens."

"Watch us do it, Dad," said Sandy. "ABC's cameras are here. Cross your fingers and hold your breath 'til it's over."

"We'll be watching," they all chimed and signed off with a rousing "Good-bye."

Time had ticked away. We needed to pack our duffles, pin our hair in chignons, stop at the coffee shop for Anasazi soup and maybe chew on a black cricket candy.

"Remember to take an eye-liner pencil and glue for our nails," said Sandy. "We'll do our faces at the pool."

I began to wind up for the competition. Jetés, pirouettes, and arabesques busied my legs during packing. I stomped flat footed about the room, doing the goose neck. Then in front of the mirror, I raised and lowered my arms, repeating our choreography.

"You're with it, Jacobs," said Sandy. "I'm convinced you are half Siamese."

When we were ready to go, Sandy opened the door and I flew into the hall like a soaring sea gull.

We arrived at the natatorium about seven o'clock. ABC's sports arena was ready for action. Walls were draped with patriotic bunting and America's flag hung from the top of the diving platform. Potted flowers flanked the trophy table. The winner's platform, a pyramid of three steps on each side, was carpeted in blue. Eight lanes of placid water lay waiting for me to do my thing.

Hurrying in the direction of the dressing room, Sandy said, "Because of television, this meet will begin on time. Let's catch the opening remarks on the big screen in the locker lounge."

The lounge was filled with swimmers, some half dressed and some ready to perform. Anxious as kids for a recess, we cheered when the announcer said, "Please stand for the national anthem."

Sandy and I spotted Jerry, front and center, the only redhead in the balcony.

It was nail-biting time for Sandy and me, but we needed fingernails to complete our costumes. I couldn't twist or twine my hair because every single lock was nailed to my scalp with pins. Only a thin coat of vaseline remained for me to apply to my head.

The sportscaster announced duet number one from Texas. Boisterous noise-making followed. Cheers of "yippie, yah-hoo, and tie 'em up" filled the air. A sign saying 'howdy, folks' was shown by the camera.

"Come on, partner," said Sandy. "We have to warm up. The new millennium championships are off and rolling."

The Conner twins joined us for exercises. We followed them through their Macarena moves in exchange for our grunt and groan pretzel poses. Without music to set the tempo, the twins' moves were perfectly synchronized. It was like watching your own shadow. One was the image of the other. Their flawless workout caused my lips to repeat quietly, "Double trouble. Double trouble," as I headed for my dressing cube.

We spent the next half hour primping, painting our faces, and outlining our eyes. After Sandy finished my face, I felt enchanting. She handed me a pair of dangles for my ears and said, "Here's the final touch. These go with the band of jewels your mom designed."

Standing face to face in our skintight lycra gold lamé suits, we admired our costumes and assumed the character of Siamese goddesses.

Mrs. Z came hurriedly into the locker room to raise our Oriental spirits from the salt flats to the mountain peaks.

"You will be pleased with the national judges on the panel," she said, convincingly. "Two are teachers of dance, two are past synchro champions, and there are three top-notch coaches. Swimming eleventh and after the twins, will leave room for us to slip in. With a little bit of luck, you girls will take home what the miners rushed out here to find. I'm due back at the scoring table and you are on in five minutes, so I'll see you shortly on deck. Appear with poise, confidence, and your best execution, one more time."

Hugging both of us, she left in haste.

I was ready to leap out of my skin as Coach Zavitz left our dressing room. What was about to happen next gave me thrilling chills. I nibbled at my nose clip, squeezed One More Time under my arm, and fought off the jitters with deep breathing. I heard the clerk call, "Routine eleven, report to the music room."

Automatically, my legs wanted to flutter-kick to victory.

"This is it, partner," said Sandy. "Mrs. Z's serious business is about to be tested. Let's check the music and wait for our introduction."

As we entered the music room, the clerk gasped a breath and in a climbing voice, said, "You girls look dazzling in those suits. You'll enamel the water with gold."

Hearing "March of the Siamese Children" sent me into action just as it had back home in the library. The clerk watched my pantomime, nodded her head in approval, while forming the letter "O" with her fingers.

The announcer's voice sounded like God himself speaking to his heavenly host.

"Routine number eleven, please take your position."

Sandy was first to enter the pool room, and I was right behind her. Voices in my head sang out as I walked the deck. Surging through my brain came, anything is possible, think elite, and don't bomb your first championship. Believing I was Sandy's ace partner, I repeated to myself, "Siamese, if you please," while walking like a Miss America dressed in a swim suit that fit like Saran Wrap and glittered like my pet fish.

The whistle blew and we began. After finishing our deck dance, we sliced into the water. From then on I felt relaxed. Five minutes of glory and five minutes of oceans of motions were supercalafabulistic. High above the water, with an eggbeater strong enough to support one-half of my weight, I posed for the camera. As we finished it was obvious we were the audience's favorite. People jumped to their feet. Sparty swung like a trapeze and Mrs. Z's mouth opened wide.

Sandy and I climbed out of the pool wearing smiles broad as the Pacific Ocean. We waited to hear our scores.

"Nine-point-six, nine-pont-eight, and the remaining scores are ten," said the announcer.

Sandy knew the emotional feeling of success.

"Keep calm, partner," she mouthed. "Wait for the scores for synchronization."

"Nine-point-seven, nine-point-nine, and the remaining scores are ten," came the voice from the microphone.

Salty tears began to stream down my cheeks and I flew into the arms of Coach Zavitz, hugging and soaking her uniform.

The announcer called for a ten-minute recess to give television a commercial break.

Sandy, Mrs. Z, and I wrapped in a hug and fell sideways into the pool. Mrs. Z, gurgling and sputtering, pronounced our fate.

"YOU ARE THE CHAMPS! The remaining entries can't catch you."